T.P

Welcome to the J̶̶̶̶̶̶̶̶̶̶̶̶̶̶̶̶̶̶̶̶̶̶̶̶̶̶̶̶̶ ̶̶̶̶̶̶̶̶̶̶̶̶̶̶̶̶̶̶̶̶̶lequin Presents!

This month be sure to catch the second installment of Lynne Graham's trilogy VIRGIN BRIDES, ARROGANT HUSBANDS with her new book, *The Ruthless Magnate's Virgin Mistress.* Jessica goes from office cleaner to the billionaire boss's mistress in Sharon Kendrick's *Bought for the Sicilian Billionaire's Bed,* and sexual attraction simmers uncontrollably when Tara has to face the ruthless count in *Count Maxime's Virgin* by Susan Stephens. You'll be whisked off to the Mediterranean in Michelle Reid's *The Greek's Forced Bride,* and in Jennie Lucas's *Italian Prince, Wedlocked Wife,* innocent Lucy tries to resist the seductive ways of Prince Maximo. A ruthless tycoon will stop at nothing to bed his convenient wife in Anne McAllister's *Antonides' Forbidden Wife,* and friends become lovers when playboy Alex Richardson needs a bride in Kate Hardy's *Hotly Bedded, Conveniently Wedded.* Plus, in Trish Wylie's *Claimed by the Rogue Billionaire,* attraction reaches the boiling point between Gabe and Ash, but can either of them forget the past?

We'd love to hear what you think about Presents. E-mail us at Presents@hmb.co.uk or join in the discussions at www.iheartpresents.com and www.sensationalromance.blogspot.com, where you'll also find more information about books and authors!

Private jets. Luxury cars. Exclusive,
five-star hotels. Designer outfits for every
occasion and an entourage of staff to see
to your every whim....

In this collection, ordinary women step
into the world of the superrich and are

He'll have her, but at what price?

Kate Hardy

HOTLY BEDDED, CONVENIENTLY WEDDED

TAKEN BY THE
MILLIONAIRE

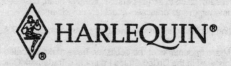

HARLEQUIN®

TORONTO • NEW YORK • LONDON
AMSTERDAM • PARIS • SYDNEY • HAMBURG
STOCKHOLM • ATHENS • TOKYO • MILAN • MADRID
PRAGUE • WARSAW • BUDAPEST • AUCKLAND

If you purchased this book without a cover you should be aware
that this book is stolen property. It was reported as "unsold and
destroyed" to the publisher, and neither the author nor the
publisher has received any payment for this "stripped book."

ISBN-13: 978-0-373-12793-1
ISBN-10:   0-373-12793-6

HOTLY BEDDED, CONVENIENTLY WEDDED

First North American Publication 2009.

Copyright © 2008 by Kate Hardy.

All rights reserved. Except for use in any review, the reproduction or
utilization of this work in whole or in part in any form by any electronic,
mechanical or other means, now known or hereafter invented, including
xerography, photocopying and recording, or in any information storage
or retrieval system, is forbidden without the written permission of the
publisher, Harlequin Enterprises Limited, 225 Duncan Mill Road,
Don Mills, Ontario, Canada M3B 3K9.

This is a work of fiction. Names, characters, places and incidents are
either the product of the author's imagination or are used fictitiously,
and any resemblance to actual persons, living or dead, business
establishments, events or locales is entirely coincidental.

This edition published by arrangement with Harlequin Books S.A.

® and TM are trademarks of the publisher. Trademarks indicated with
® are registered in the United States Patent and Trademark Office, the
Canadian Trade Marks Office and in other countries.

www.eHarlequin.com

Printed in U.S.A.

All about the author...
Kate Hardy

KATE HARDY lives on the outskirts of Norwich, England, with her husband, two small children, a dog—and too many books to count! She wrote her first book at age six, when her parents gave her a typewriter for her birthday.

She had the first of a series of sexy romances published at twenty-five, and swapped a job in marketing communications for freelance health journalism when her son was born, so she could spend more time with him. She's wanted to write for Harlequin since she was twelve, and when she was pregnant with her daughter, her husband pointed out that writing medical romances would be the perfect way to combine her interest in health issues with her love of good stories.

Kate is always delighted to hear from readers—do drop in to her Web site at www.katehardy.com.

For Chrissy and Rich—the best aunt and uncle
in the world—with love.

CHAPTER ONE

'RUN that by me again.' No way could Isobel have heard him correctly. She was used to Alex asking if he could sleep on her sofa while he was in London between digs or on a flying visit—his own flat in London was let out to tenants—but this request...

She must've been hearing things.

'Will you marry me?' Alex repeated.

Exactly what Isobel thought he'd said.

Was this some kind of joke?

Unlikely, because he looked serious. Besides, Alex didn't make that kind of joke. She frowned. 'I don't understand. Have you gone temporarily insane, or something?'

'No. I just need to get married. And I think you'd be the perfect wife.'

Oh, no, she wouldn't. She'd already failed spectacularly with Gary. 'You get women posting their knickers to you. You could get married to any woman you wanted.'

He laughed. 'They don't post their knickers to me, Bel. That's a vicious rumour started by Saskia.'

Saskia was Alex's baby sister and had been Isobel's best friend since they were toddlers. Though Isobel wasn't so sure the comment was just sibling teasing. 'I know for a fact you get asked out by more women than most men even dream about.'

'Women who fantasise about The Hunter—not about me.'

'You're one and the same, in their eyes.' In hers, too: Alex had presented three series of a popular television archaeology programme, based on a series of articles he'd written for a leading Sunday newspaper, and when Isobel had curled up to watch the programmes she'd thought he came across just as he was in real life. Clever and extremely well read, but with a bit of flamboyance that had women dropping at his feet and the kind of easy charm that meant he made friends effortlessly and couldn't go anywhere without half a dozen people hailing him by name. It had been like that even before he'd been catapulted to fame as 'The Hunter', an explorer who delved in ancient places and found treasure; but nowadays, with national television exposure, he was recognised by people he'd never even met.

'Just let it slip to one of your gossip-column friends that you're looking for a wife and there'll be queues for miles,' she suggested.

'Gossip-column journos aren't anybody's friends except their own,' he corrected. 'And none of those women would be like you—sensible and settled.'

She coughed. 'You're digging yourself deeper into that hole, Alex.' He wanted to marry her because she was *sensible?* Give her a break. That wasn't why people got married.

Then again, marrying for love hadn't exactly worked for her, had it? Her marriage hadn't survived its final crisis.

'Why do you need to get married anyway?' she asked.

'Because I need to get a job.'

'This is beginning to feel like *Alice Through the Looking Glass.* The harder I try to understand this, the weirder it seems.' She shook her head. 'Apart from the fact that you don't need to get married to get a job, why do you even need a job in the first place? You're loaded.'

Alex waved a dismissive hand. 'It's got nothing to do with money.'

'So what, then?'

'It's complicated,' he hedged.

She leaned back against the sofa. 'You're not getting out of it that easily, Alex. Explain. Why do you need to get married?'

'Because of this job. It's perfect, Bel—Chief Archaeological Consultant for a firm that works with all the big property developers. When the developers plan to build on a site and discover remains of some structure they hadn't even known existed, or we already know there are remains in the area that need to be conserved or recorded before any development work can start, I'd be in charge of a team of archaeologists who'd excavate the site.'

'A desk job, you mean?' She shook her head, scoffing. 'No way. You'd last five minutes before you came down with a case of terminal boredom.'

'It's not a desk job. I'll be doing the initial site visits and setting up the exploration, liaising with planning officers and talking people into giving us more time than they really want to for excavation work. Plus I'd be talking to the press, explaining the significance of the find.'

Put that way, it sounded just the sort of thing he'd enjoy doing. Alex would love the chance to be the first one in maybe hundreds of years to discover something. And the time pressure to excavate the site as thoroughly but as quickly as possible, so the builders could finish their job on schedule, would just add to the thrill for him. He thrived on being too busy.

'I still don't understand why you need a job. Aren't you going to do the Hunter stuff any more?'

'Of course I am.' He shrugged. 'But it's only for a few weeks a year.'

She understood where he was coming from. Alex was a workaholic—it was the only way to explain how he managed to pack more into two days than the average person did in a working week—and he liked it that way. 'In other words, not enough to keep you busy and out of mischief.'

He laughed. 'Exactly. I could do more TV work, I suppose, but I've talked to my agent and I agree with him that over-exposure would be a mistake. It's better to keep the series the length it is and leave people wanting more, rather than them seeing my face and thinking, Oh, no, not *him* again, and switching off. So I need something else to keep me occupied.'

'What about your articles?'

He shrugged. 'As you say, a desk job would drive me crazy. I need something with a lot of variety.'

'Lecturing, then? If you had tutorial groups as well, that'd give you the variety because your students would all be different.'

He wrinkled his nose. 'I've had offers, but to be honest I don't really want to teach.'

Isobel frowned. 'What's wrong with what you do now?'

'Nothing. I love freelancing. But I'm thirty-five, Bel. I need to be realistic about the future. In ten or twenty years I'm not going to want to spend hours at a time on my knees in a trench in the pouring rain. So I want to make the right career move now, while all my options are still wide open.'

It was a fair point, although Isobel thought Alex had enough strength of personality to make his own opportunities. She had a feeling there was a bit more to it than what he was telling her, but she couldn't work out what. A relationship that had gone wrong? Surely not, because Alex kept his relationships light and very casual and in all the years she'd known him she couldn't remember a girlfriend lasting more than half a dozen dates.

Maybe she was asking the wrong questions.

'I still don't understand where the married bit comes in.'

'Apparently, the guy who owns the company wants a married man for the job.'

She snorted. 'No way. That's discrimination. It's against the law, Alex.'

'They're not going to be able to ask me outright about my marital status,' he agreed. 'But it seems the last two guys they hired lasted all of six weeks before they got an offer they couldn't refuse for—I quote—a really glamorous dig abroad.'

They both laughed, knowing that real archaeology wasn't glamorous in the slightest. The stuff Alex did on TV accounted for a tiny fraction of the hard graft behind the scenes, and certainly didn't take account of being on your knees in a muddy trench for hour after hour, or the long gaps between finds.

'So third time around they want someone settled,' he continued. 'The word is they're looking for someone who'll commit to the project for at least two years. And, you know as well as I do, a married man's seen as more dependable than a single guy because he's already made a commitment.'

She flinched. 'Marriage doesn't always mean commitment.'

He winced. 'Sorry, honey. I didn't mean to rip open old wounds.'

'I know you didn't.' Alex didn't always think. Mainly because he did things at a hundred miles an hour and his head was stuffed full of the past—just like her own. Which was one of the reasons why she'd always got on so well with him.

He took her hand and squeezed it briefly. 'But you know what I mean. My reputation's going to count against me. The Hunter, a gypsy vagabond.'

She rolled her eyes. 'You're hardly a vagabond, Alex.' Even though he did have itchy feet and didn't tend to stay long in one place.

'But I'm part gypsy. My mother says I'm a throwback to her grandfather—'

'Who met your great-grandmother when she accompanied your great-great-grandfather to a dig in Egypt in the nineteen twenties, and your great-grandfather fell in love with her,' Isobel finished. She knew the story, and she'd always privately thought it really romantic.

Archaeology was in Alex's blood. And so too was the gypsy heritage. Which was why 'The Hunter' was his perfect screen persona: dressed in jeans with a white shirt, and a battered Akubra hat worn at a rakish angle, Alex Richardson made women swoon. That and his dark curls, his hair worn slightly too long, his exotic olive skin, and those piercing light grey eyes, completely unexpected with the rest of his colouring.

'Look, I've spent the last few years travelling the world. On digs or for the show, admittedly, but still travelling.'

'Which shows commitment to your job,' she pointed out.

'It's not *enough*.' He shook his head in apparent frustration. 'The series played me up as the sort who won't obey orders—a maverick who'll go his own way regardless.'

She couldn't argue with that. Besides, that was exactly what Alex was like—not that there was any point in telling him.

'So that's why I need a wife. To prove I'm settled.'

'I still think it's a crazy reason to get married. And why ask *me*?'

'I already told you. Because you're settled.'

That stung, and she couldn't help sniping, 'You mean I'm staid and boring.'

He laughed. 'No. Just I've known you for ever. You're the girl next door.'

'Strictly speaking, I haven't lived next door to you since I was thirteen and you went to Oxford,' she said dryly. 'Which is the best part of seventeen years ago.'

'You were still there when I came home for the holidays,' he reminded her.

The girl next door. As familiar as wallpaper. Alex hadn't noticed her as a *woman*.

At her continued silence, he sighed. 'Look, I never planned to get married. Archaeology's my life—just as the museum is yours. There isn't room in my life for another relationship.'

She raised an eyebrow.

He winced. 'Sorry, Bel. That came out wrong. Mouth in gear, brain not. What I mean is, if I'm going to get married, I want to marry someone I like a lot. Someone I've got a lot in common with. Someone I trust.'

It should've warmed her that he felt that way about her. Trusted her. Liked her a lot. Exactly the way she felt about him. But she couldn't help asking, 'What about love?'

He lifted one shoulder in a half-shrug. 'I don't believe in it.'

She knew where he was coming from. She didn't believe in love any more, either. She'd loved Gary, but it hadn't been enough to make their marriage work. Though at the same time, marriage without love seemed...wrong, somehow. 'All three of your sisters are married,' she remarked. 'And if they weren't happy and in love with their husbands—'

'I'd take their husbands apart,' he admitted. 'Very slowly. And remove their hearts with a rusty spoon.'

Although Alex rolled his Rs and his eyes, she wasn't sure that he was being entirely dramatic.

'But it's different for the girls.'

Sexism? From Alex? Now that she hadn't expected. 'Since when did you turn into a chauvinist?'

He frowned. 'I'm not. It's got nothing to do with gender. Just that…' he lifted one shoulder in a half-shrug '…I'm not like them.'

'So this marriage business—you're looking for someone you like, someone who shares your interests, and who's not going to tie you down.'

'I'm not planning to have a string of girlfriends or be unfaithful to my wife, if that's what you're asking.'

Alex dated a lot. Which meant he had a lot of sex. If he was giving that up…did that mean he was planning to have sex only with his wife?

With *her*?

Oh, Lord.

The last twelve years suddenly unravelled, back to when she'd been eighteen and Alex had kissed her. Just once. But what a 'once' it had been. He'd actually taken her breath away. For one mad moment she'd thought that Alex had noticed her—that instead of seeing her as just his little sister's best friend, the girl he'd known for years, he'd seen her as a soul mate. Someone who shared his interests. Someone he was attracted to. And then she'd realised he was being kind. Showing her that just because her rat of a boyfriend had dumped her, it didn't mean that she'd never be kissed again.

He'd even said as much. Said that she'd soon find someone else. Added that she had a whole world to conquer.

That kiss hadn't meant the same thing to him as it had to her. And Isobel was pretty sure things hadn't changed since then. Alex saw her as a friend—a close friend, but *just* as a friend.

So no way would this marriage work.

She couldn't do it.

She'd already ended up in one loveless marriage, and she really couldn't face starting another on the same basis. She dragged in a breath. 'I'm sorry, Alex. I can't marry you.'

CHAPTER TWO

ALEX schooled his features into neutral. 'Why not?'

'Because it's wrong to get married without loving each other.'

He flapped a dismissive hand. 'Of course I love you, Bel.'

'But not in *that* way, Alex. And I'm not putting myself through that again.'

Alex stared at her. 'Hang on. Are you telling me Gary didn't love you? That he was unfaithful to you?'

She shook her head. 'He didn't break his marriage vows, no. Let's just leave it that our marriage turned into a mess.'

She looked uncomfortable, and Alex knew Isobel wasn't telling him the whole story—but he also knew not to push her. She'd talk to him when she was ready. She always had.

'Though it didn't take him very long to find someone else.' Isobel dragged in a breath. 'His new partner's just had their first baby.'

That had clearly hurt her. He'd never asked Isobel why she'd split up with Gary—because it wasn't any of his business and he didn't want to rake open any painful wounds—but he'd always supposed that Gary had wanted a baby and she hadn't been prepared to make any comprom- ises with the career she loved.

So had his guess been completely wrong? Was Isobel the one who'd wanted children?

No, of course not. She adored Saskia's daughter, Flora— her god-daughter and Alex's niece—but Alex had always assumed that it went with the territory of being Saskia's best friend. Isobel liked children, otherwise she wouldn't have been able to do her job—but she really, really loved what she did. A museum interpreter who worked with hands-on exhibits, dressing up as a Roman matron during school holidays or at weekends and giving cookery demonstrations and showing people what everyday life was like in Roman Britain, as well as working behind the scenes as a curator on the exhibitions that toured other museums.

So if it wasn't the baby, maybe she was upset because the baby signalled that things were well and truly over between her and Gary. That they could never go back to how things were.

According to his sister, Isobel had rarely dated since her marriage ended two years ago, so maybe she was still in love with Gary. Alex had never thought Gary was good enough for her—for starters, the man had a feeble handshake and no imagination—but he also didn't like seeing Isobel hurt and miserable. 'Come here.' He slid his arms round her and held her close. 'I'm sorry.'

'What for?'

'That it didn't work out for you. That he let you down.' He stroked her hair. 'I know it's probably not what you want to hear, but he was never good enough for you.'

'But he didn't ask me to marry him just because I'm staid and sensible.'

Alex pulled back slightly and looked her in the eye. 'I asked you because I want this job and being a married man is going to give me the edge I need.'

'Rubbish. You can talk your way into anything.'

'Apart from getting you to marry me, you mean,' he parried. 'And you didn't let me finish. Whatever I said about you being sensible—which you are—the main reason I asked you is because you're my friend. I've known you for years and years. I enjoy your company and I trust you. And that's a much, much stronger basis for a marriage than being "in love" with someone.' Thinking of Dorinda, Alex curled his lip. She'd been his biggest mistake ever. And she'd taught him all about the misery of love. A lesson that meant he wasn't going to repeat that mistake. 'Being "in love" is just temporary. It's hormonal. Whereas what we've got has a much more solid foundation and it's not going to change.'

'Isn't it? Because that's what worries me, Alex.' She bit her lip. 'I don't want to lose your friendship when it all goes pear-shaped.'

He sighed. 'Apart from the fact that it's not going to go pear-shaped, things aren't going to change between us.'

'How do you know? Unless you're talking about a marriage in name only—and as you said you weren't planning to have a string of girlfriends, I have to assume you're...' Her voice tailed off and she actually blushed.

He'd never seen her colour like that before.

And even though he knew he wasn't playing fair, he couldn't resist teasing her. 'Assume what, Bel?'

'That getting married means having sex with each other.' Her flush deepened.

Alex felt as if his skin were suddenly burning, too. *Sex with Isobel.* Right now, he was holding her. Loosely, admittedly, but he was still holding her. All he had to do was move forward a fraction, dip his head, and he could kiss her.

His mouth went dry.

He could remember the last time he'd kissed her, other than

the usual peck on the cheeks that accompanied their welcoming hugs when they hadn't seen each other for a while. The night she'd come round to their house, crying her eyes out because her boyfriend had dumped her for someone more glamorous and less studious, and he'd answered the door. Saskia had been out, so he'd taken Isobel into the summer house in their garden for a heart-to-heart. He'd told her that the boyfriend was an idiot and it didn't matter because there was a whole world out there just waiting for her to conquer it.

And he'd kissed her.

Just once.

Before remembering that Isobel was eighteen to his twenty-three, much less worldly-wise, and he really shouldn't be kissing her like that.

Now he wondered what would've happened if he'd kissed her a second time. Would they have ended up making love in the summer house? Would he have been the one to introduce her to the pleasures of love-making?

And what shocked him even more was that his body was reacting even now at the thought of it.

Making love with Isobel.

He became aware that she was speaking.

'And besides, I'm not your type.'

'I don't have a type,' Alex protested.

'Yes, you do. You always go for tall, skinny brunettes with legs up to their armpits.'

'You have dark hair.' The colour of a chestnut that had just slipped out of its prickly case, it was soft and silky when he ran his fingers through it. 'And you're not short.' She was curvy rather than skinny, though with three younger sisters he knew much better than to discuss a woman's weight or body shape.

'I'm five feet four. That makes me slightly shorter than the average woman.'

He smiled at her. 'It also makes you two inches taller than the average Roman woman in the fourth century.'

She rolled her eyes. 'Trust *you* to know that.'

He laughed. 'Actually, you were the one who told me. When you were researching your first talk about Roman women.'

She stared at him in obvious surprise. 'You remember that?'

'Course I do. We must have sat up half the night talking about it. Well, after I'd bored the pants off you with all those photographs of the dig I'd just come back from.'

'I wasn't bored.'

'See? We have things in common. Lots of things. And we like each other. Getting married would work, Bel.'

The colour was back in her cheeks, even deeper this time. 'Supposing we're not, um, compatible?'

'Compatible?'

'In bed,' she muttered. 'What if I'm rubbish at sex?'

'If that's what Gary said, he clearly wasn't doing it right— and his ego made him blame you.'

'Mmm.'

'Look at me, Bel,' he said softly. She had huge brown eyes that had topaz glints when she laughed, and a perfect rosebud mouth. Why had he never really noticed that before? 'I think we'd be…' he paused as his heart gave an unexpected kick '…compatible.'

'I can't believe we're even discussing this!' She pulled back from him. 'So why didn't you ever get married, Alex?'

He let her go. 'Because my job meant a lot of travelling— and that meant either living apart from my wife most of the time, or dragging her around the world with me. Neither option's a fair one.'

'And you never met anyone who made you want to stay in one place?'

Once, but that had been a long time ago. In the days when he'd still worn rose-coloured glasses. Before he'd discovered that Dorinda was a liar and a cheat and had played everyone for a fool, including him. Since then, he'd never quite been able to trust anyone. He'd held back in his relationships, unwilling to risk his heart again and have it ground beneath a stiletto heel. Keeping things light and fun had worked for him, until now. 'I told you, I don't believe in love. But I do believe in friendship. In honesty. And if you marry me, Bel, I'll be a good husband to you.' A much better one than Gary had been.

'I can't get married. Ask someone else.'

There wasn't anyone else he'd trust enough to marry. He shrugged. 'Look, forget I asked. Come on, I'm taking you out to dinner.'

'Why?'

He rolled his eyes. 'It's not an ulterior motive. You've said no and I'm not going to bully you into saying yes. Bel, you're putting me up for a few days, so taking you out for dinner to say thank you is the least I can do.'

'Alex, you don't need to do that. You know I never mind you staying here.'

He smiled. 'I know. But I like having dinner out with you. I like talking history and arguing over interpretations and laughing too much and eating half your pudding—because I'm greedy and you're always nice to me.'

She rolled her eyes. 'You're impossible.'

'Uh-huh.' But to his relief she was smiling and relaxed with him again. 'Is that Moroccan place we went to last time still open?'

'I think so.'

'Good. Let's go.'

* * *

It always surprised Isobel slightly that Alex liked taking the tube rather than a taxi. Then again, on the tube people were careful not to catch anyone's eye, so although he'd probably be recognised it was unlikely that someone would ask for an autograph or a photograph with him taken with the camera on their mobile phone. Besides, without the hat, people were more likely to think he was a guy who just happened to look like the archaeologist from the show, rather than being the man himself.

It was practically impossible to talk on the tube; there were just too many people squashed onto the train. During late spring and summer, rush hour seemed to last a lot longer; the office workers crushing onto the train were quickly replaced by tourists.

Isobel wasn't sure whether it made her more relieved or uptight—or both at the same time. Relieved, because she didn't have to make eye contact or conversation with Alex. And uptight, because it gave her time to think about what he'd said.

Getting married—to Alex.

Having sex—with Alex.

Oh, Lord.

She'd enjoyed her friendship with Alex. She always had. And she'd married Gary because she'd loved him.

But a little bit of her had always wondered: what if Alex hadn't had his string of glamorous girlfriends? What if he'd repeated that kiss when she was twenty-one? What if she'd ended up with Alex instead of Gary?

Panic skittered through her. She had to be insane even to be considering this. Marriage wouldn't work. She'd had one serious relationship before Gary, so she was hardly experienced—whereas Alex had practically had a girlfriend at every dig, not to mention the ones in between. She'd never be able to live up to his expectations.

His words echoed in her head. *I enjoy your company and I trust you. And that's a much, much stronger basis for a marriage than being 'in love' with someone.*

Was he right? Were friendship and trust a better basis for a marriage than love and desire? Should she have said yes?

A note appeared in front of her eyes. In Alex's spiky, confident handwriting.

'Stop brooding. "Dinner" means dinner.'

The last word was in capitals and underlined three times. She faced him. Sorry, she mouthed.

He smiled, and it gave her a weird sensation—as if her heart had just done a somersault. Which was anatomically impossible and completely ridiculous. Especially as, at the age of thirty, she was way, way past the teenage heartthrob stage.

And then it was their stop.

The crowds of people swirling round them meant it was still impossible to talk. But she was aware that Alex was behind her on the escalator. So close she could have leaned back against him.

What would it be like to feel Alex's arms round her?

What would it be like to feel his hands against her bare skin?

What would it be like to feel his mouth touching her body intimately?

'OK?' he asked when they were through the ticket barrier and standing outside on the street.

'Fine.'

'Liar.' He caught her hand and squeezed it briefly.

The lightest contact...and it sent a shiver all the way through her. Woke nerve-endings she'd forgotten she had.

No.

It wasn't possible for her to feel like this about Alex. And even thinking about it meant she was storing up trouble for herself. She'd loved Gary. Deeply. But it hadn't stopped everything going wrong. So she had to keep some kind of distance between herself and Alex, not let her heart get involved.

Or her libido.

'I'm not lying,' she mumbled, but she didn't look him in the eye until they got to the Moroccan restaurant.

Alex insisted on holding the door open for her. 'I don't care if it offends your feminist nature. It's good manners and it's how I was brought up,' he informed her.

It was how she'd been brought up, too. 'Thank you,' she said, meaning it.

Stepping inside the restaurant was like stepping out of London and into a souk. The air smelled of cinnamon and cardamom, and the décor was as beautiful as she remembered it; the walls were painted shades of saffron and terracotta and deep red, there were rich silks everywhere, the wrought iron chairs were covered with bright silk cushions toning with the walls, and the silk hanging from the ceiling gave the place the effect of being in some rich prince's tent. Tea-light candles flickered on the glass tabletops, and rose petals were scattered everywhere.

The waiter ushered them to the table and handed them each a menu.

'Red wine OK with you?' Alex asked, glancing down the menu.

'Fine.'

'Good. *Meze* to start, I think. Anything in particular you fancy?'

'I'll let you choose.' Not that she wasn't capable of choosing her own meal, but she knew how much Alex enjoyed it. And, as he'd said, his tastes were very similar to her own, so she knew she'd like whatever he chose.

'What do you want for your main course?'

'Chicken tagine. The one with preserved lemons.'

'I think I'll have the same. We'll choose pudding later,' Alex decided.

And after pudding…he'd go home with her.

And if she'd said yes to his proposal, he would have taken her to bed. Proved how compatible they were.

Her concentration went completely, and she was reduced to saying, 'Mmm,' and nodding in the right places as Alex talked to her about the dig he'd been on in Turkey before his return to London. And it was even worse when the *meze* arrived—a selection of dishes to share. Traditionally, Moroccan food was eaten with fingers and pitta bread was used to scoop up the dips, and every time she reached for one of the stuffed vine leaves or the aubergine and cumin dip or the felafel, her fingers brushed against Alex's. In the past, it wouldn't have bothered her, but tonight the lightest contact made her tingle. A sensual awareness that spread through every part of her body and made her wish that she'd been wearing a thick concealing sweater rather than a thin T-shirt that revealed her body's reaction to his touch.

If Alex said one word about being able to see her nipples, she'd kill him.

She ate her chicken tagine in silence.

And then Alex sighed.

'Would it really be so bad?'

'What?'

'Going to bed with me.'

She felt the colour shoot into her face. 'Alex!'

'You've been quiet ever since I suggested getting married.'

And having sex. 'It's just…I never thought about you in

that way before.' It wasn't the strict truth, but she didn't want him thinking that she'd been secretly lusting after him. Their friendship had been genuine.

'Not ever? Not even when you were...I dunno... eighteen?'

When she was eighteen? The only time she remembered him kissing her on the mouth. 'No.' She looked curiously at him. Did he remember that, too? And was he saying that, all those years ago, he had seen her as more than just the girl next door? 'Did you?'

'Not when I was eighteen—of course not.' He flapped a dismissive hand. 'Bel, you were still a child when I was eighteen. And when you were eighteen and I was twenty-three, there was still a huge gap between us.' He paused. 'But now you're thirty and I'm thirty-five. The gap's not there any more.'

She knew she was going to regret asking, but she couldn't help the question. 'And?'

'And...' he paused '...I'm thinking about you in that way right now.'

There was a gleam in his eyes she'd never seen before. A purely masculine gleam that told her he was interested in her. As a woman, not as a friend.

Her breath hitched. 'Oh.'

'You're thinking about it, too, aren't you?' he asked, his voice sounding husky.

'Yes,' she admitted, before she could stop herself.

'Good,' he said softly. 'Hold on to that thought.'

It still seemed like some weird parallel universe. The idea of becoming Alex's lover. Yesterday it would've been un-thinkable. Today...the possibilities sent heat all the way down her spine.

She found it hard to concentrate when the waiter offered

them the dessert menu, and eventually went for the safe option: *bagrir*, a light pancake served with honey and ice cream and nuts. Alex, just as she could have predicted, went for the selection of chocolate and cardamom ice cream.

'Oh, yes. Best ever,' Alex said when he tasted it. 'Open your mouth.'

Oh, Lord. The pictures that put in her mind.

It must have shown in her expression, because she saw colour bloom along his cheekbones. 'I meant, you have to try this. And it's the cardamom one—I know you loathe chocolate ice cream.'

So he wanted her to lean forward and accept a morsel from his spoon? But her T-shirt was V-necked. Leaning across the table would give Alex a full-on view of her cleavage.

The thought made her nipples tighten even more.

'Bel, it's melting. Hurry up.' He held the spoon out towards her.

She leaned across the table. Opened her mouth. Let him brush the cold, cold spoon against her lower lip before she ate the morsel of ice cream.

'Good?' he asked.

She had a feeling he didn't mean just the ice cream.

'Good,' she whispered.

He smiled—a warm, sensual smile that made her catch her breath.

'My turn,' he said.

They'd done this so many times before—shared a pudding, tasted each other's meals, filched buttered toast from each other's plates or a swig from each other's mug of coffee with an ease born of long familiarity.

But tonight it was different.

Tonight they were feeding each other like lovers.

And when he ate the proffered piece of her *bagrir*, she could see that he looked as distracted as she felt.

She had no idea how they got through the rest of their dessert, or the mint tea afterwards. Or when Alex had ordered a taxi, because one was waiting for them outside practically as soon as he'd paid the bill.

He didn't say anything on the way back to her flat; he simply curled his fingers round her own—reassuring and yet incredibly exciting at the same time.

Holding hands with Alex was something she'd never really done. She was used to him giving her a friendly hug—almost a brotherly hug. But there was nothing remotely fraternal in the way he was holding her hand right at that moment. His touch was gentle—and yet firm enough so that she could feel the blood beating through his veins, in perfect time with her own.

When the taxi pulled up outside her building, Alex paid the driver and opened the car door for her. Isobel's hands were shaking slightly and she fumbled the entry code for the security system; it took her three goes to press the right buttons in the right order. By the time she unlocked her front door, she was a nervous wreck.

Alex paused, leaning against the doorway. 'Bel, let me reassure you that I'm planning to sleep on your sofa tonight. I'm not going to push you into anything you don't want to do.'

That was what worried her most: what she wanted to do. The more she thought about sex with Alex, the more she was tempted to do it.

Except she didn't want to risk ruining their friendship.

And she definitely didn't want to tell him her deepest, darkest secret—the thing she'd only told Saskia after extracting a promise from her best friend that Saskia wouldn't tell anyone else and wouldn't ever talk about it again.

She couldn't possibly marry Alex. Even though she was

pretty sure he didn't want children, what if he changed his mind? If anyone had asked her before today, she would've said straight out that Alex would never get married. And yet today he'd asked her to marry him. Tomorrow he might want to start a family. Something she wasn't sure she could do.

Her worries must have shown on her face, because he said softly, 'Have I ever let you down before?'

'No.'

'That's not going to change.'

Maybe. But if she married him, she'd be letting him down. Taking a choice away without telling him. Which was morally wrong.

Even though she knew she was being a coward, she muttered, 'I've got a bit of a headache. I need an early night.'

'I'll make sure I don't disturb you. Do you want me to bring you a glass of water and some paracetamol?'

'Thanks, but I'll manage. I'd better sort the sofa bed out for you.'

'I'll do it.' He reached out to stroke her cheek. 'See you in the morning, Bel. Hope you get some sleep.'

CHAPTER THREE

TRUE to his word, Alex didn't disturb her. And when Isobel got up the next morning he'd already put the sofa bed back to rights, tidied up and made coffee.

'Morning. How's your head?'

'Better, thanks.' The fib had blossomed into the truth, and she'd ended up taking paracetamol.

'Here.' He passed her a mug of coffee—hot, strong and milky, exactly the way she liked it. 'Toast?'

'Yes, please.' She sat down at the little bistro table in the kitchen. This was the Alex she knew best. Her friend who knew her so well that he could practically read her mind. Though usually she was the one making toast and he was the one filching it from her plate.

'So what are you doing today?' he asked.

'Roman kitchens,' she said. 'How about you?'

He joined her at the table after he'd switched on the toaster. 'A bit of research.'

But nothing that really excited him, from the flatness of his tone. And he still seemed faintly subdued when she left for work.

Alex really needed a new challenge, she thought. Like the job he'd told her about yesterday; his eyes had been almost pure silver with excitement when he'd described it. But she still didn't see how getting married would make any difference to whether he got the job. There was no reason for her to feel even slightly guilty about turning down his proposal. She'd done the right thing for both of them.

Though she couldn't stop thinking about him all day. And when she walked in her front door that evening and smelled something gorgeous cooking, guilt bloomed. 'Alex, I didn't expect you to cook for me.'

'No worries.' He shrugged. 'It's as easy to cook for two as it is for one.'

She scoffed. 'You mean, you were that bored.'

He handed her a glass of red wine. 'Go away and let me have my mid-life crisis in peace.'

'It's my flat. I'm not going anywhere.' But she sat down at the table. 'What mid-life crisis? Alex, you're thirty-five. That's hardly middle-aged. And you don't have a conventional desk job, so you can't exactly take a six-month sabbatical and grow your hair and ride a motorbike round the world in search of adventure. That's what you *do* for a day job, for goodness' sake!'

'I don't have a motorbike.'

'Don't nit-pick. What I mean is, for you to do the opposite of what you normally do, you'd have to cut your hair short and get an office job and wear a suit and date the same person for more than three consecutive evenings. For most people, your life would be an adventure.' She looked at him. 'What mid-life crisis, anyway?'

He wrinkled his nose and turned away to pour himself a glass of wine. 'Just forget I said anything.'

She shook her head. 'You've been quiet for you, today. Something's obviously bothering you. Come and sit down and talk to me.'

'I'm busy cooking dinner.'

She sniffed. 'Chicken casseroled in red wine, baked potatoes and salad?'

He smiled wryly. 'All right. So most of the cooking's already done. How did you know what I was cooking, anyway?'

'Apart from the fact it's your signature dish? Educated guess,' she said dryly. 'You just emptied that bottle into a clean glass.'

'I could've been swigging straight from the bottle,' he pointed out.

They both laughed, then he shrugged. 'Anyway, I've been quiet because this is what happens when I have too much time on my hands. I start thinking—and that's dangerous.'

'Talk to me, Alex,' she said softly. 'What's wrong?'

'This is going to sound mad.'

'Tell me anyway.'

He sighed and joined her at the table. 'I'm thirty-five, Bel. My little sisters are all settled, married with a family. All the people I was at university with have settled down—some of them are on their second marriage, admittedly, but they're settled. And although I love my life, I'm starting to wonder if what I've got is really enough for me any more. If it's what I really want.'

'So you're saying you want to settle down and have children?' Isobel asked carefully.

'Yes. No. Maybe.' He took a sip of wine. 'I suppose what I'm saying is that I'm starting to think about what I do now. I'm doing something about my job, but what about the rest of my life? Do I want be one of these eternal bachelors who still behave as if they're in their twenties when they're pushing sixty?'

She smiled. 'I can't quite see you doing *that*, Alex.' He'd still be immensely charming when he was almost sixty. He'd still turn heads. But he'd also have dignity and wouldn't try to pretend he was still young.

'But time goes by so fast, Bel. It seems like yesterday that Helen had the boys, and now they're seven. Next thing I know, I'm going to be forty-five and I'll be the spare man invited to dinner parties to make up the numbers, sitting next to the woman who's just got divorced and either hates all men or is desperate for company.'

She frowned. 'Alex, this isn't like you. And this whole thing about looking to the future…oh, my God.' A seriously nasty thought clicked into place. The reason why he suddenly wanted to settle down. 'Is there something you're not telling anybody?'

'Such as?'

Well, if he wasn't going to say it, she would. This needed to be out in the open. Right now. She swallowed hard. 'You're seriously ill?'

For a moment, there was an unreadable expression on his face, and Isobel felt panic ice its way down her spine. Please, no. Not this.

'I'm fine. In perfect health,' he told her. 'But I did hear some bad news about a close friend while I was on my last dig.'

Someone else. Not Alex. Relief flooded through her, followed by a throb of guilt. Bad news was still bad news. 'I hope your friend's OK now.'

He shook his head. 'He didn't make it. It didn't seem right, standing at Andy's graveside only a couple of years after I'd been in that same church for his wedding. He's the first one of my friends to die, and it's made me realise how short life can be. How I shouldn't take things for granted. And I got to thinking, maybe it's time I did something about settling down.' He looked thoughtful. 'That's one of the things I really liked about the specifications for this job. There's enough travelling to stop me getting itchy feet, but not so much that I can't have a family life as well. It's the best of both worlds.'

A family life.

So he *did* want children.

Which meant, Isobel thought, that he needed to marry someone who could definitely have children—not someone who had a huge question mark hanging over her. After her miscarriages, the doctor had reassured her that the statistics were all on her side, that plenty of women went on to have healthy babies afterwards. Miscarriages were so common that the hospital wouldn't even begin to look into the causes until a woman had had at least three.

But Gary hadn't wanted to take the risk. He hadn't wanted to stick around and wait.

And although Alex wasn't like Gary—she knew he had the integrity to stand by her—he wanted a family. Something she might not be able to give him.

Telling him the truth was out of the question. If she did, she'd see pity in his face and she'd feel that she was no longer his equal. No way did she want that to happen.

But not telling him… If he was serious about settling down, if he'd meant that proposal and intended to ask her again, she'd have to refuse. It wouldn't be fair to accept. If it did turn out that she couldn't carry a baby to term, that she couldn't have children…she didn't want their relationship to go the same way as her marriage had. Down the tubes.

She pushed the thoughts away. This wasn't about her. It was about him. 'Hey, you'll be a shoo-in for the job. And once you actually stay in one place for more than three seconds, you'll find Ms Right,' she said brightly.

She suppressed the wish that it could've been her.

They spent the rest of the evening talking shop, the way

they always did. And Alex behaved the next morning as if everything was just fine, so she followed his lead and pretended he hadn't opened his heart to her, the previous night.

She'd been at her desk for an hour when a courier arrived.

Odd. She wasn't expecting a delivery. But when she opened the parcel, she discovered a box of seriously good chocolates. And there was a note in familiar spiky script: *'Thanks for listening.'*

Alex might be a whirlwind, but he never took anything for granted.

She flicked into her email program.

Thanks for the chocs. Unnecessary but very, very nice. Bel x

A few moments later, her monitor beeped. Mail from Alex.

Least I could do. Don't eat them all at once.

Ha. As if she would. She smiled, and carried on with the report she was writing.

A few moments later, her monitor beeped again.

Doing anything tonight?

Nothing special. Why?

It was a while before he responded. And then:

Consider your evening annexed. Meet you from work. What time do you finish today?

Six. Do I need to change first?

If you're dressed as Flavia, yes! Otherwise, fine as you are. Ciao. A x

Which told her absolutely nothing about what he had planned. Typical Alex.

But she was busy and it was easier to go along with him, so she didn't push the issue.

He was waiting for her in the foyer at six, wearing a casual shirt and dark trousers and looking absolutely edible. For a moment, her heart actually skipped a beat.

But this wasn't a date. This was just two friends meeting up while one of them was briefly in London. The fact that he was staying with her was by the by. They weren't living together and it wasn't that kind of relationship.

And that marriage proposal hadn't been a real one. She really needed to get a grip.

'Hi.' His smile did seriously strange things to her insides, and she strove for cool.

'Hi, yourself. Good day?'

'Not bad.' He slid a casual arm round her shoulders and ushered her down the steps. 'How was yours?'

'Fine.' She was glad her voice wasn't as shaky as she felt. This was crazy. She and Alex had always had a tactile relationship. So how come this didn't feel like his usual hug?

'Good. You hungry?'

She grinned. 'Considering I've been eating chocolate all day…'

'What, and you didn't even save one for me?'

She laughed. 'No. But I did share them in the office.'

'Hmm. So was that a yes or no to food first?'

'Food before what?'

'Before…' He took his arm from her shoulders, fished in his pocket for his wallet, then removed two tickets and handed them to her.

She felt her eyes widen. Two tickets to that evening's performance of *Much Ado about Nothing* at the Globe. The best seats in the house. 'These are like gold dust, Alex!' And to get them at short notice he must've paid a fortune to one of the ticket agencies.

'I wanted to see the play, and it's more fun going with someone who actually enjoys it, too.'

'At least let me pay for my own ticket.'

'No. But you can buy me a drink in the interval, if you insist.'

'I do insist.'

'"My dear Lady Disdain,"' he teased.

'I did that play for A level,' she reminded him.

'I know.' He rolled his eyes. 'I used to have to listen to you and Saskia murdering it in the summer house when I was home in the holidays.'

'Murdering it?' She cuffed his arm. 'I'll tell her that, next time I talk to her. And then you'll be in trouble.'

'No, I won't. I'm her favourite brother.'

'Her only brother,' Isobel corrected.

'Still her favourite,' Alex said. 'So. Food first or later?'

She glanced at her watch and at the time on the ticket. 'Better make it later. Unless you want to grab something from a fast-food place?'

'I'd rather wait and have something decent.'

'Later it is, then.'

The tube was so crowded again that they didn't get a chance to talk on the way over to Southwark. And the bar at the Globe was so crowded that they were forced to sit incredibly close together to have any chance of hearing each other speak.

Odd.

Alex was used to touching Isobel—giving her a hug hello and a kiss on the cheek when they said goodbye—but this was different. Now, he was aware of her in another way. Of the softness of her skin. Of the sweet scent of her perfume—a mixture of jasmine and vanilla and orange blossom. Of the shape of her mouth.

And it shocked him how much he suddenly wanted to kiss her.

'Alex?'

'Sorry. It's a bit noisy in here. I can barely hear you.' Acting on an impulse he knew was going to land him in trouble, but he was unable to resist, he scooped her onto his lap.

'Alex!'

She was protesting—but she slid one arm round his neck to stop herself falling off his lap.

'It's easier to hear you if you talk straight into my ear,' he said, his mouth millimetres from her own ear. 'That way you don't have to shout. And I don't get backache from leaning down to you.'

She cuffed him with her free hand. 'That's below the belt.'

And maybe this hadn't been such a good idea. Because the whisper of her breath against his ear sent a peculiar sensation down his spine. A feeling he really didn't want to acknowledge.

He took refuge in teasing. 'I apologise... Shorty.'

'Huh.' She rolled her eyes.

He knew she wasn't upset with him; this was the kind of banter they'd always indulged in. The kind of banter that was safe because their friendship was deep and it had been practically lifelong.

When she'd finished her glass of wine, he glanced at his watch. 'We'd better find our seats.'

'Sure.' She slid off his lap, and Alex was shocked to discover he actually missed the warmth of her body against his.

The production was fantastic. And as soon as Benedick

spoke his 'dear Lady Disdain' line, Alex glanced at Isobel—
to see her glancing straight back at him. He curled his fingers
round hers, acknowledging that he knew what she was remembering. To his pleasure, she didn't pull away. But all the
way through the play, when Beatrice and Benedick were
fencing verbally, he found himself thinking of himself and
Isobel.

*'I do love nothing in the world so well as you. Is not that
strange?'*

His fingers involuntarily tightened for a moment round hers.
This was crazy.

Of course he wasn't in love with Isobel. She was his *friend*.

But it didn't alter the fact that he was holding her hand.
Treating this like a date, when it wasn't one at all.

He needed to regain his composure.

But for the life of him he couldn't let her hand go.

At the end of the play, he released her hand so they could
clap. And his arm was only round her on the way out of the
theatre so he could protect her from the crowds.

At dinner afterwards, they chatted animatedly about the
play until their meal arrived.

'Next time we'll have to take Saskia as well,' he said. 'And
Mum—if she's up to it.'

'How is she?' Isobel asked.

'You know my mother. She almost never admits to feeling
under the weather.' He sighed. 'This lupus thing... I worry
about her.'

Isobel reached across the table and squeezed his hand.
'She'll be fine, Alex. Saskia was telling me about it—I know
they haven't found a cure for lupus, yet, but they can keep it
under control with medication.'

'But it's going to take a while for them to find the right
treatment to help her.' Alex grimaced. 'I've read up on it. I

was in Turkey when Helen rang me and told me—and although I came home straight away, a snatched weekend here and there isn't enough. I need to be around a bit more. Living in the same country as my family would be a start.' He smiled wryly. 'I'm not planning to move back in with my parents, because I'm used to doing things my own way and I'd drive them crazy, not fitting in with their routines—but I want to do my bit. It's not fair to leave everything to the girls. I'm the oldest, and our parents are *my* responsibility.'

Isobel raised an eyebrow. 'I think your parents would say they're their own responsibility.'

'Maybe.' Alex frowned. 'Mum's putting a brave face on things but I know she hates it when I'm away so much, and she worries every time she turns on the news and hears of some kind of political unrest which might be somewhere near wherever I am at the time. It's extra stress she doesn't need.'

'Alex, it's not your fault she's got lupus.'

'No?' He raised an eyebrow. 'It's stress-related.'

'And my money's on most of the stress being caused by her job. Saskia says she's been feeling a lot better since she changed her hours and went part-time.'

'Even so, it doesn't help if she's worried about me.'

'She'll be pleased about your new job, then,' Isobel said.

'Hey, I'm not quite arrogant enough to count my chickens—I know I'm in the running, but if they decide that my career to date makes me too much of a risk, that I'll stay in the job for all of five minutes and then leave them in the lurch when I get a better offer...' He shrugged. 'Well, something else'll turn up.'

She frowned. 'Alex, do you actually have to be married to make them think you're settled, or would being engaged be enough?'

He thought about it. 'Engaged would probably be enough.'

* * *

Alex needed her. And of course she wanted to help him. He was too proud to ask her again, she knew, so there was only one thing she could do. 'Alex. I want to help you. I really want you to get this job and be happy.' She took a deep breath. If she got engaged to him, it wasn't the same as being married, was it? It wasn't the same as tying him down to someone who might not be able to give him what he wanted in life. 'Look, if we get engaged—after you get the job we can quietly break off the engagement and go back to being how we are now.' And because they weren't getting married, she wouldn't have to tell him the truth about herself—about the miscarriages. Everything would be just fine.

'You'd get engaged to me?'

'Until you get the job, yes. If it'd help.'

She could see the relief in his eyes. 'Thank you, Bel. I really appreciate this.' He took her hand, raised it to his mouth and kissed her palm before folding her fingers over where his lips had touched her skin. 'Any time I can return the favour, do something for you, you know I will.'

'Hey. That's what friends are for,' she said, striving for lightness despite the fact that the touch of his mouth had sent desire zinging through her veins.

Though his words made her heart ache. Yes, there was something Alex could do for her. But it wasn't going to happen, so there was no point in even letting herself think about it. A real marriage and babies weren't on his agenda. Besides, the fact that Gary had a baby now proved that the problem was with her, not him.

'To you,' Alex said, lifting his glass. 'My lucky charm.'

'What was that you were saying about not counting your chickens?' she asked wryly.

'With you by my side,' Alex said, 'I could conquer the world.'

Oh, help. He sounded serious. She reverted to some childhood teasing. 'Alexander the Great, hmm?'

He laughed. 'Hey. I'm not going to make you change your name to Roxana. Though if you really want to…'

'No, thanks!'

'And this is an engagement of convenience.'

'Exactly. Until you get the job. Which you will.' She raised her own glass. 'To you.'

'To us,' he corrected. 'And to teamwork.'

'Teamwork,' she echoed.

CHAPTER FOUR

ALEX spent the weekend in the Cotswolds visiting his parents, and Isobel was shocked at how much she missed him, how empty the flat seemed without him.

Don't get too used to this, she warned herself. Alex would move out once he'd got the job and decided where to settle. If he decided to move back to his own flat, he might stay for his tenants' notice period, but he wouldn't stay any longer than that. And their engagement was one of convenience, which wouldn't last very long; there was no point in getting a ring.

She went out for a long walk on Hampstead Heath on the Sunday; when she let herself back into the flat, she was surprised to see Alex already there. And she was furious with herself for the fact that her heart actually missed a beat. 'You're back early,' she said, keeping her voice deliberately light.

He looked grim. 'Mmm.'

There was only one thing she could think of that would've made him look so upset. 'Is your mum all right?'

'She's fine.'

'Then what's wrong?'

He raked a hand through his hair. 'Things didn't go quite according to plan.'

'How do you mean?'

He sucked in a breath. 'I took my parents out to lunch today. I was telling Mum about the job—and that you'd agreed to be my temporary fiancée, to give me the right profile. Except she didn't hear the word "temporary".' He sighed deeply. 'She thinks we're really getting married, Bel. And her face… She looked so happy. As if a huge weight had been lifted from her. I just didn't have the heart to correct her—not in the middle of the Partridge, anyway. I was going to wait until we were back home and then explain without having an audience listening in. But then I got out of the car and Dad was shaking my hand and slapping me on the back and telling me how pleased he was that I was finally settling down and about time it was too—and the next thing I knew, my mum had already gone next door to see your mum.'

Isobel blinked. 'Marcia told my mum we were engaged?'

'And Saskia. And Helen. And Polly. And half the street. I've only just managed to persuade her not to stick a notice in the local paper.' He looked rueful. 'I tried to ring your mobile to warn you, but your voicemail told me your phone was unavailable—and your landline went straight through to your answering machine.'

'I went out for a walk—I must've been in a bad reception area.'

'I sent you a couple of texts. Maybe they went AWOL.'

Or maybe she'd accidentally left her phone in silent mode. She took it out of her bag and checked the screen. There were three messages from Alex, all telling her to ring him urgently and not to listen to any of the messages on her answering machine until he got back to London.

She glanced at the answering machine. 'Messages.' The light was still flashing, so clearly he hadn't listened to them.

'I'm really sorry, Bel.'

'Better find out what they have to say.' She pressed 'play'. The first message was from Alex. 'Houston, we have a problem. Call me when you can—and if you've got other messages on the machine after this, don't take any notice of them, OK? I'll explain everything when I get back.'

Next was her mother. 'Bel, Marcia just told me. It's fantastic news—but why didn't you tell me yourself, love? Get your diary and call me when you're back. Your dad and I want to take you both out to dinner to celebrate. Love you.'

Then it was Alex's mother. 'Bel, we're so pleased to hear the news—I wish Alex had waited until you were back from your course, so you could've told us together, but I know what my son's like. He can't wait for anything. See you soon, love. And we're *so* pleased. We couldn't have hoped for a better daughter-in-law.'

And then Saskia. 'Oh, my God, you're actually going to be my sister! Isobel Martin, how could you keep something like *this* quiet? And from *me*, of all people! Ring me the second you get this. I want *details*.' She laughed. 'And congratulations. This is brilliant. It's the best news I've heard all year.'

Isobel sat down and looked at Alex. 'Oh, blimey. They're all so pleased.'

'I know.'

'And *what* course? Why does your mother think I'm on a course?'

He lifted a hand in protest. 'She asked why you weren't with me to share the news. I had to think on my feet. So I said the first thing that came into my head—that you were on a course. Which I know was a lie, and I know you hate lying, but what else could I do?'

'You could've told them the truth.'

'How?' He sighed. 'I've been racking my brain all the way

here to work out how to fix this. Look, if you don't mind going along with it for a while, then we can say I've done something terrible—I dunno, got drunk and disgraced you and gone off with another woman at a party or something— and you can break off the engagement in high dudgeon. And then we can just go back to normal.'

She shook her head. 'Alex, that's a hideously bad idea— it'll hurt everyone. Your parents will never forgive you if they think you've treated me badly, mine will never forgive you either, and it'll cause rifts all over the place. And I'm not going to tell even more lies. It's enough of a mess as it is.'

'Bel, you heard them all. They're delighted that we're together. It's as if we've given them Christmas, a milestone birthday and a huge lottery win all rolled into one. If I tell them the truth, they'll be so disappointed, so upset that it's not happening. At least if we tell them it didn't work out, it'll let them down gently.'

'By you being unfaithful? That's hardly being gentle, Alex.'

'Then I hope you've got a better idea, because I can't think of any other way.'

Her mind had gone completely blank. 'I can't, either,' she admitted.

'Mum said she wondered how long it would take me to see what was right under my nose, and she's glad I finally realised.' He raked his hand through his hair. 'She thinks I've been in love with you secretly since for ever.'

'Of course you haven't.' Isobel shifted guiltily. Though could she say the same for herself? The fact that she could still re- member how a kiss had felt twelve years ago...' This is crazy.'

'And it's my fault. I'm sorry, Bel.' He looked grim. 'I'm just going to have to call everyone and put them straight. I apologise if it's going to cause any awkwardness for you.'

'Hey. I'll get over it,' she said lightly.

'I just hate bursting Mum's bubble. Especially as Saskia called me on my way back here and told me it's the brightest she's heard Mum sound in months.'

'I know where you're coming from. My parents have wanted to see me settled down again, too, after Gary. I think it's because they're...' She bit her lip. 'I was a late baby. Their only one. And although Mum's a young seventy-two, she's been talking lately about...' She swallowed. 'About getting old.'

'And the fact that they're your only family.'

Trust Alex to see straight into the heart of things. And to voice what she couldn't bring herself to say—that when her parents died she'd be completely on her own.

He paused. 'You know, this could be a solution for both of us.'

'What could?'

'Getting married. For real.'

It was a moment before she could speak. 'But, Alex, you said you want to settle down and have a family.'

He shrugged. 'A wife counts as family.'

'So you don't want children?'

He spread his hands. 'Bel, if you want children, that's fine by me—if you don't, that's also fine. No pressure either way.'

'But...' Panic skittered through her. If only he knew. They might not have a choice. 'We can't do this.'

'Yes, we can.' He took her hand. 'Think about it. Our parents get on well. I like your parents and you like mine—we're both going to have great in-laws.'

Something Isobel definitely hadn't experienced with Gary, whose mother had always resented her. Nothing had ever been said overtly, but there had been plenty of pointed comments; Gary's mother hadn't taken well to the idea of his wife being the most important woman in his life. Isobel knew she wouldn't have to put up with anything like that from Marcia, who had always treated her as a much-loved part of the family.

'Both lots of parents are going to be relieved we're settled down,' Alex continued, 'and they'll stop worrying about us and nagging us. And we've got the basis for a brilliant marriage—we like each other.'

'But liking isn't *enough*,' she protested.

'Yes, it is. It's better than love, Bel. It's honest. It's permanent—something that's not going to change and we don't have all these false ideals and rosy-coloured glasses, so we're not going to get hurt. We're going into this knowing exactly what we're doing. Eyes wide open.'

'I…'

He sighed. 'Bel, if you're worrying about what I *think* you're worrying about…there's only one way to prove it to you.' He bent his head and kissed her.

It was the lightest, sweetest, most unthreatening kiss, and Isobel felt herself relax. Alex cupped her face in both hands and bent his head again. His mouth moved against hers, soft and sweet and gentle.

And then suddenly it was as if someone had lit touch-paper and heat flared between them. Her hands were fisted in his hair, their mouths were jammed together, and his tongue was exploring hers.

She couldn't remember the last time she'd wanted someone so much.

And it was as scary as hell.

He broke the kiss for a moment, just to warn her, 'Stop thinking—just feel.' And then he was kissing her again, making her head spin.

The next thing she knew, Alex had swung her up in his

arms and was carrying her to her bedroom. He set her down on her feet next to the bed. 'Wow, Bel, you're a real hedonist. I've never seen so many pillows.'

Of course. It was the first time he'd ever been in her bedroom. He'd always slept on her sofa bed whenever he'd stayed over at her flat. He walked over to the wrought-iron footboard and ran his fingers along it. 'This is beautiful. And I'm very glad you have a double bed.' He smiled. 'Especially because you have all those pillows.'

'I read in bed,' she said defensively. 'It's more comfortable with lots of pillows.'

'Other things are better with lots of pillows, too,' he remarked.

And when colour shot into her face he laughed, stole another kiss, and went over to her bedside table. He switched on the lamp, closed the curtains, then frowned. 'This light's a bit bright.'

'I told you, I read in bed.' She rolled her eyes. 'I don't see the point of giving myself eye strain.'

'True. But I want something softer. Don't move. And whatever you do, don't start thinking.'

'Why?'

He sighed. 'Because… Look, there's an easier way.' He walked back over towards her, slid his arms round her and kissed her—sensual, demanding, and it actually made her knees weak. She couldn't remember ever feeling this turned on by just a kiss.

'Whatever's put that look in your eyes, hold that thought,' he said, his voice huskier and deeper than usual.

He left the room and she could hear him moving things in her living room. He returned a few moments later with the pillar candle she kept on her mantelpiece, placed it on the bedside table next to the lamp, lit the candle and then switched off the lamp.

'Better,' he said in approval.

Then he sat on the bed and patted the space next to him. 'Come here,' he said, his voice soft.

'Alex, I…' How could she tell him she was scared she'd disappoint him? That she was out of practice? That no way would she match up to the leggy stick insects he normally dated?

In the end, she didn't have to, because he took her hand and tugged her towards him, then scooped her onto his lap. 'It's going to be OK, Bel. And you don't have to be shy with me. I've seen you naked before.'

She stared at him in surprise. 'Since when?'

'When you were about…oh, I dunno. Two? It was a really hot summer that year and we almost always had the paddling pool out. You and Saskia used to splash about all afternoon.' He laughed. 'Mum's probably got a photo somewhere.'

When she was *two?* She rolled her eyes. 'That doesn't count.' But she found herself laughing, relaxing.

'That's better,' he said softly. 'Stop worrying. This is going to be fine.'

And if she were honest with herself, it was something that had been simmering between them for years. Unfinished business. An attraction she'd never admitted to because she'd been so sure Alex didn't think of her in that way…but he'd brought it up himself a few days ago. Told her that he saw her as a woman.

Maybe—just maybe—this was what they both needed.

To get it out of the way and go back to being sensible.

Though there was still a problem. She took a deep breath. 'Alex, I haven't done this for a while.'

'Good.'

'Good?' Now that was a reaction she hadn't expected.

He smiled, and rubbed the pad of his thumb against her

lower lip. 'Very good, in fact. Because it means I get to remind you what pleasure's all about.'

When her lips parted involuntarily, he dipped his head again to kiss her; by the time he broke the kiss, her head was spinning. He slid his hands under her T-shirt, stroking her abdomen with the tips of his fingers. 'Your skin's so soft.' He nuzzled the curve of her neck. 'You smell of orange blossom. I want to touch you, Bel. I want to look at you.' Gently, he tugged at the hem of her T-shirt and she let him pull the material over her head.

He sucked in a breath. 'You're beautiful. How come it's taken me all these years to notice?'

'Because you've dated a string of women who were practically models?' she suggested.

He gave her a mock-affronted look. 'Isobel Martin, are you calling me shallow?'

'Yup.'

He grinned. 'Better hope I have hidden depths, then.'

He traced the lacy edge of her bra with the tip of one finger. The light touch made her quiver, and her nipples were tightening again.

Although he didn't make a comment, he'd clearly noticed, and rubbed the pad of his thumb across them; the friction of her lacy bra against her sensitive skin sent a thrill through her.

'You're still fully clothed,' she said.

'Do something about it, then,' he invited.

She undid the buttons of his shirt to reveal a broad, muscular chest, olive skin and dark hair. Such perfect musculature. She ran her fingertips over his hard pectoral muscles, his ribcage. And when she looked him straight in the eye, she could barely see his irises, his pupils were so huge. Meaning that he was as turned on by this mutual exploration as she was.

He slid the straps of her bra down, then kissed her bare shoulders; Isobel felt a sharp kick of excitement in her stomach. His mouth drifted along to the curve of her neck; when she closed her eyes and tipped her head to one side, he began a trail of tiny, nibbling kisses all the way along the sensitive cord at the side of her neck. His lips were warm and sure and incredibly sexy, and he was finding erogenous zones she hadn't even known existed. Isobel shivered when he lingered in the sensitive spot behind her ear and her mouth parted involuntarily.

Then she became aware of the lacy fabric of her bra falling away from her skin; he'd unfastened it with one hand, so deftly she hadn't even realised what he was doing. And now her breasts were spilling into his hands; he cupped them, lifting them slightly, teasing her nipples with his thumb and forefinger and making her quiver with arousal. From the hard pressure through his jeans against her thigh, she knew that he was just as turned on.

'I love having you sitting on my lap,' he whispered, 'but it isn't enough for me, Bel. I need more. *Now.* I need to touch you. Taste you.'

She needed it, too. 'Yes.'

Gently, he shifted her off his lap and lay her back against the pillows. Kneeling between her parted thighs, he dipped his head, took one nipple into his mouth and sucked.

Oh, Lord.

So many sensations at once.

The soft silkiness of his hair against her skin, contrasting with the beginnings of spiky stubble on his face. The movement of his tongue and lips. The warmth of his mouth. The pressure of the suction. The tingling that started in her nipples and seemed to flood through every nerve-end.

'Oh, yes, Alex,' she whispered, arching her back against

the softness of the duvet. She slid her hands into his hair, wanting more.

He lifted his head a fraction and looked up at her, his eyes dark in the candlelight. 'Do you like that?'

'Yes.' The word came out slurred with pleasure.

'Good. So do I.' He paid attention to her other nipple, teasing it with his teeth and his tongue until she was wriggling, then slowly kissed his way down her abdomen. 'I wish you were wearing a skirt.'

'Why?'

'Because these are in the way.' He stroked his hands down the denim of her jeans, then slid one hand between her thighs, cupping her sex through her jeans. 'If you were wearing a skirt I'd be closer than this.' He rubbed one finger along the seam of her jeans, pressing against her clitoris. '*Much* closer.'

And right now she needed him much closer. She shivered. 'Alex. You're driving me crazy.'

'That's the idea.' He shifted back onto his haunches, keeping his gaze firmly fixed on hers as he undid the top button of her jeans.

They were getting nearer and nearer the point of no return.

Slowly, slowly, he lowered the zip. The air felt cool against her heated skin, and she shivered.

'Cold?'

'And hot,' she admitted.

'Good.' He leaned forward and kissed the skin he'd just uncovered. 'And you're going to get hotter still by the time I've finished with you.'

And wet.

God, she was wet. So ready for him.

Gently, he encouraged her to lift her buttocks, and pulled her jeans down over her hips. He made short work of removing them after that, taking off her socks at the same time so she was left wearing only a tiny pair of knickers. He looked at her, lying against the pillows, and sucked in a breath. 'Wow. How come I never noticed you're a pocket Venus? All curves.'

Curves. She flushed and wrapped her arms round herself.

He groaned. 'I didn't say "fat".'

'I am compared with the stick insects you normally date.'

'I might date them,' he said softly, 'but it doesn't necessarily mean I sleep with them. And, for the record, I happen to *like* curves. And yours are gorgeous.' He slid the tips of his fingers underneath hers. 'Don't be shy with me. I want to see you, Isobel.' Gently, he prised her hands away from her body. 'You're lovely.'

She dragged in a breath. 'This isn't fair. You're still wearing your jeans.'

'I'm all yours, honey. Do with me what you will.' He spread his hands in invitation.

It had been a long, long time since she'd played this sort of game with anyone. Towards the end, with Gary, sex had been primarily to make a baby, not an expression of love. And when that had all gone wrong...

'Touch me, Bel,' he said, his voice sinfully inviting.

Isobel reached out and undid the top button of his jeans. And the next. And the next. She could feel his erection straining against her fingers as she continued unbuttoning his fly. What was sauce for the goose, she thought with an inward smile, and traced the outline of his penis with one fingertip.

He shivered. 'I think I should warn you not to tease me.'

'Is that a threat?'

He shook his head. 'You can tease me as much as you like, later. But I want this first time to be for you.' He took her hand and kissed it, sucking each fingertip in turn.

The movement of his mouth against her skin made the pulse beat hard between her legs. If he could make her feel like this just by playing with her fingers, what was it going to be like when he touched her more intimately?

She sat up again and pulled his jeans down over his hips. On impulse, she pressed her mouth against his abdomen.

He groaned. 'I warned you about teasing me.' He rolled to one side and ripped off his jeans and socks, then joined her on the bed.

'I half expected you to go commando.'

He laughed. 'No.' Then his expression went serious. 'Bel, just for the record, I don't sleep around. I date a lot, I have a good time, but I'm fussy about who I take to bed. And in the past I've always used protection.'

She nodded, appreciating his candour. And she believed him absolutely. 'I haven't—' she dragged in a breath '—slept with anyone since I split up with Gary.' Two years. More, if you counted the last disastrous months of her marriage. She'd dated a couple of times but she'd never gone further than a goodnight peck on the cheek.

He stroked her cheek. 'Then we'll take this slowly.'

He was going to stop? Now?

She must've said it aloud, because his eyes darkened. 'I'm not going to stop, Bel.' His voice was deep and husky and sexy as hell. 'And, as much as I feel as though I'm going to implode if I'm not inside you in the next nanosecond, I want this to be good for you.'

He wanted her that much? Oh-h-h. 'I need you inside me, too,' she whispered. And she couldn't remember the last time she'd felt that needy. The last time she'd wanted sex for its own sake and not to make a baby.

Gently, Alex removed her knickers and slid one hand between her thighs. She felt the long, slow stroke of one finger against her sex, a movement that had her quivering and needing more. As if he could read her mind, he did it again. And again.

'This is taking it slowly?' She could hardly get the words out.

'Uh-huh.'

'You're driving me crazy, Alex. I want…'

'This?' He pushed one finger inside her.

She gasped. 'Yes.' The word came out as a hiss of pleasure.

He continued circling her clitoris with his thumb, and she wriggled against him, wanting more.

'You're so warm and wet for me,' he whispered. 'Just how I want you.'

'Alex. Now. Please,' she said huskily. 'I need… I want…' Why couldn't she even string a sentence together? She was never this inarticulate.

He smiled. 'Guess what? I want you all the way back.' He stripped off his jockey shorts, then took a condom from his discarded jeans and rolled it on before kneeling between her thighs again and kissing her. She felt the tip of his penis nudge against her entrance—and then he was inside her with one long, slow, deep thrust.

She shuddered.

He stilled, letting her body adjust to his. 'Are you all right, Bel?'

'Yes—I just wasn't expecting this to… Oh-h-h,' she said as he began to move again.

She could feel the pressure growing, warmth curling at the soles of her feet and spreading up through her body into ripples, then waves.

She'd known Alex would be good at this—Alex was good at everything he did—but she really hadn't expected it to be this good, taking her to a completely different world.

'Bel,' Alex demanded softly. 'Look at me.'

She opened her eyes—and saw the same wonder she was feeling reflected in his own eyes as her climax hit her.

It was a while before she could even think, let alone speak. And she was cradled in Alex's arms, her head resting on his shoulder.

'I think,' he said softly, 'that proves we're pretty compatible.'

'Yes.' More than she'd ever expected.

He stroked her face. 'So. We like each other. We have a lot in common. And the sex is good.'

She had a nasty feeling she knew where this was heading.

'So how about we don't burst anybody's bubble?' He shifted so he could kiss her lightly. 'If we get married, it's going to solve all the problems at a single stroke.'

No, it wasn't. Because she was going to have to tell him about the miscarriages. 'Alex—about the baby business…'

'It's fine.' He pressed his forefinger lightly against her lips. 'Stop worrying. I know you love your job and you're good at it. I'm not expecting you to give it up. If we do have children, we'll work something out. If we don't, then we'll carry on exactly as we are.'

He said that now, but how would he feel later?

'It's a win-win situation.'

Hardly. Because Alex didn't love her. Which meant their marriage would be one-sided—and if he had any idea that she was falling in love with him, he'd back off straight away. He made no secret about the fact he considered himself allergic to love.

'Bel. Stop panicking.' He stole a kiss. 'It's going to be fine.'

'Is it?'

He smiled. 'I think I'm going to enjoy spending the rest of today proving it to you. Very, very slowly.'

Her face felt hot. 'Alex!'

'I'm going to get us something to eat.' He climbed out of bed. 'Stay put. And I mean it, Bel. No worrying. This might just be the best idea either of us has ever had.'

CHAPTER FIVE

THE alarm shrilled; Isobel rolled over to hit the snooze button and collided with a body.

A warm, hard and very obviously male body.

'Good morning, Bel,' Alex said quietly.

How could he possibly be awake already? They'd spent much of the previous night making love, after Alex had returned to bed with a platter of fruit and cheese and crackers and insisted on feeding her. They'd explored each other's bodies so completely that neither of them had anything left to hide.

And right now all Isobel wanted to do was snuggle back under the duvet, wrapped in his arms, and go back to sleep.

'Hello? Earth to Isobel? Anyone home?' he teased.

He sounded bright and chirpy. But that was Alex, able to burn the candle at both ends. He could stay up late—or, in the case of last night, spend a fair part of it making love—and still be wide awake and ready to go at the crack of dawn.

'Uh,' she said.

He must've hit the snooze button because the alarm stopped shrieking; then he rolled her onto her side and curved his body round hers. 'Good morning, sleepyhead.' He kissed the sensitive spot behind her ear. 'I take it you have to be up for work this morning.'

'Uh.'

He chuckled. 'I always thought you were a morning person.'

'I am,' she mumbled, 'if I get enough sleep first.'

He traced a lazy circle round her navel with his fingertip. 'Ah. That. I guess we were a bit…busy, last night.' His hand flattened against her stomach, then slid upward to cup one breast. 'Any regrets, this morning?'

Apart from aches in muscles she'd forgotten she had… She twisted round to face him and pressed a kiss into his chest. 'No.'

'Good. So you're going to marry me, then.'

He hadn't actually asked her, the previous night. None of the traditional down-on-one-knee stuff, no declaration of love, no four little words.

She suppressed the sting of hurt. He *had* asked her, a few days before—and she'd refused him. So this time round he hadn't asked and she hadn't accepted. Which, in a weird sense, made them quits in this marriage that wasn't a marriage.

'Bel?'

She forced herself to sound light-hearted. 'Depends.'

'On what?'

'I need coffee.'

'I can take a hint.' He laughed. 'Go and have a shower, and I'll make us some breakfast.' He stroked her hair. 'I'm tempted to join you in the shower…but then you'd be seriously late for work, and I don't want to get you into trouble.'

'Trouble?'

'For spending the morning in the shower with me instead of doing what you're supposed to be doing.'

She could just imagine the water beating down on them as Alex eased into her body, and desire flooded through her. 'Oh-h-h.'

'Tempted?' he teased.

She slid the flat of her palm down his side, curving round his buttocks. 'Mmm.'

The alarm shrilled again, and she groaned. 'I have to go to work.'

'We'll take a rain check. Just keep thinking about whatever put that incredibly sexy look on your face just now—and tell me tonight. In detail. So I can act it out.'

Oh, Lord.

How was she supposed to concentrate on anything for the rest of the day, after a promise like that?

He shut off the alarm and climbed out of bed, pausing only to pull on his boxer shorts, and headed for the kitchen.

By the time Isobel had showered and dressed for work, Alex had made a pot of proper coffee, set the table and was halfway through buttering some hot toast.

'Breakfast,' he said with a smile.

Sitting there at her kitchen table, bare-chested, he looked utterly edible.

She'd never breakfasted like this with Alex before. Sure, they'd had breakfast together plenty of times. But not when he was practically naked. And not when they'd spent most of the previous night making love, and his hair was all mussed, and she knew just what that sexy mouth felt like against her skin. All she wanted to do right now was sit on his lap, make his hair even messier, kiss him stupid and drag him back to her bed.

God, she really needed that coffee.

She couldn't fall in love with Alex. This wasn't part of the deal.

'Thanks,' she mumbled, reaching for her mug. He'd made the coffee just the way she liked it—hot, strong and milky. 'Mmm. Perfect.'

'Me or the coffee?' he enquired with a lazy grin.

'The coffee, of course.'

'Huh. Tomorrow, Isobel Martin, you can make your own breakfast,' he retorted. Though the gleam in his eye told her he was enjoying the banter as much as she was.

'House rules—you stay here, you make breakfast,' she teased back.

His eyes glittered. 'I can think of some much more interesting house rules. But then you'll be very, *very* late for work.' He moistened his lower lip. 'Want me to tell you?' His gaze slid lower. 'Mmm. Looks as if you can guess.'

She folded one arm across her breasts. 'Alex. That's not fair.'

He laughed. 'Sorry, Bel. I shouldn't tease you. Not when I can't carry it through to its proper conclusion.'

'No.' She paused. 'Alex, about last night... I wasn't expecting it to be so...' How could she say this without insulting him? 'Well, so good,' she ended lamely.

'Neither was I,' he said. 'I mean—I've always liked you. A lot. But last night wasn't just going through the motions, was it? It wasn't just perfunctory sex.' He reached over and took her hand. Kissed her palm and folded her fingers over his kiss. 'Maybe we should've done this a long time ago.'

'You weren't ready to settle down.' She wasn't so sure that he was ready now. Alex wasn't a settling-down kind of man. He was more like a meteor shower that made a spectacular appearance in your life for a brief while and then vanished—until the next time.

So although sex with Alex had been a revelation—of the nicest possible kind—she wasn't going to let her heart get involved. Wasn't going to rely on him.

'What are you doing today?' she asked.

'A bit of research. You?'

'Probably working up a handout for the touring exhibition.'

'Want to do lunch?'

She shook her head regretfully. 'Sorry. I've got meetings that I know are going to end up going through lunch.'

'Admin. Bleugh.' He pulled a face. 'My least favourite bit of any job.'

'Says the man who's planning to get a desk job.'

'I'll be negotiating for an admin assistant.'

She laughed. 'You *would*.'

'I don't want to spend my time on tedious paperwork when I could be doing something much more interesting.' He smiled at her. 'I'll see you back here tonight, then. And I might even cook you dinner.'

'Yeah, right,' she scoffed. 'Once you're in the archives, you only leave when they chuck you out at closing time.'

He gave her a speaking look. 'As if you don't do exactly the same.'

She shrugged. 'I love my job.'

'I know. Which is why you understand me so well.'

She finished her toast. 'I'd better be off. See you later.'

'You're leaving me to do the washing-up? Not fair,' he complained teasingly. 'I made breakfast.'

'I'll pay you back tonight.'

He raised an eyebrow. 'I'll hold you to that.'

Over the next few days, life just seemed to get better and better. Alex was right about an affair not affecting their friendship; he still talked to her as much, argued with her and teased her. But at the same time their love-making gave an added dimension to their relationship. One Isobel hadn't expected. She couldn't remember being this happy before, even in the early days with Gary—in the days before they'd tried for a family. Before Gary had accused her of putting her job before their baby, the last time she'd miscarried. An accusation that was so far beyond unfair, it was untrue. She'd wanted a baby just as much as he had. And if the midwife had put her on bedrest for her entire pregnancy, she would've done it for the sake of their child.

She shook herself.

Not now.

Though now she'd agreed to marry Alex, the question of babies rose uppermost in her mind. He'd been so casual about it, saying that if it happened, it happened, and he'd be guided by her. But when she told him just how much she wanted a baby, would it make him run?

And there were no guarantees she could even have a baby.

Then there was his new job. Although he was based in England, it would still involve a fair amount of travelling. So his lifestyle wasn't really going to fit in with being a dad.

She needed to talk to him about this. Before the engagement and wedding plans went too far. It was just a matter of finding the right time.

The following Thursday morning, Alex was not only up at the crack of dawn, he was wearing a suit.

Isobel blinked. 'Blimey. You really are trying to impress the interviewers.'

'No. I'm giving them a chance to see me as a consultant,' he corrected. 'Someone who can talk to the money people— they already know I can do the other side of the job.'

'The last time I saw you in a suit, it was Flora's christening.'

'It's the same suit,' he said with a grin. 'I only possess one. And it usually gets dragged out for just christenings and weddings.'

'Uh-huh. Well, you look professional. Just check your pockets for confetti.'

'Good point.' He checked his pockets. 'No confetti.'

'Good.' She kissed him lightly. 'And I'm buying you dinner tonight to celebrate.'

'You really think I'm going to get the job?'

'Of course I do. You're the best candidate.'

'You don't actually know any of the other candidates,' he pointed out.

She shrugged. 'I don't need to.'

He smiled. 'Thanks for the vote of confidence. So what are you doing today?'

'Being Flavia.'

He laughed. 'You love all that dressing-up stuff, don't you? It's just like when you and Saskia were little—pretending to be a princess or a bride or what have you.'

'Don't knock it,' she said with a grin. 'It's a lot of fun. I know you proper archaeologists have a bit of a downer on living history, but it gets the kids interested, and that's a good thing.'

'Living history's OK as long as you're not too *earnest* about it.' He rolled his eyes. 'And you know exactly what I mean. So what's today's topic? Roman food?'

'Domestic stuff. Beauty,' she said.

'Mmm. Well, if you need someone to oil you and get the strigil out…'

She laughed. 'Don't you dare. You'll mess up your suit.' She paused. 'Will you know today?'

He nodded. 'Assessments this morning and then interviews, and then they'll tell us.'

'Text me when you hear?'

'Course I will.' He glanced at his watch. 'I'd better go. See you tonight.'

'I'm not going to wish you luck. Just go and be yourself. That'll be more than enough to get you the job.'

'Especially as I'm a nice, settled, about-to-be-married man.' He kissed her. 'Thanks, Bel. I owe you.'

She patted his shoulder. 'Go and show them what you're made of.'

When he'd gone, Isobel tidied up the kitchen and then headed for work. Although she normally loved the days when she did the hands-on displays, today she found herself itching for her lunch break so she could check her mobile phone.

But there was no message from Alex. He must still be in the interview, or waiting round while the other candidates were being grilled, she thought. Well, she'd just have to wait until the end of her shift.

She was partway through getting the children to guess what all the items were on the little manicure set she kept on her belt, and was right at the point where they were gleefully disgusted by the earwax remover when she became aware of someone walking into the gallery, dressed in a toga with a broad purple stripe. Odd. She didn't think they had anyone playing the part of a senator today. Maybe they'd changed the schedules round a bit without telling her and were doing politics in the next gallery.

As the man in the toga drew nearer, she realised who it was.

He'd oiled his hair back to give the impression of a short Roman crop.

And he looked utterly gorgeous.

But what on earth was Alex doing here, dressed like this?

'Sorry I'm late. Politics in the Forum,' he said with a smile, coming to join her.

What?

But—

She didn't have time to ask any questions because he stood next to her and took her hand, before turning to the audience. 'I'm Marcus, the senator in charge of the emperor's entertainment. I order the elephants and the gladiators for displays in the circus, so I'm very busy—and I really need someone at home keeping my domestic affairs in order, running my household.'

He was ad-libbing, Isobel knew. But his knowledge of the historical period was sound and he was used to performing to a TV camera or lecturing at conferences, so their audience would no doubt think he'd played this role for years.

'One of the important customs in Roman times was betrothal. If I wanted to get married, I'd have to negotiate with my intended bride's family. And if they approved of me, we'd have a betrothal ceremony.' He produced something from inside his robe; it glittered in the light. 'The Roman wedding ring used to be made of iron in the early period, but betrothal rings like this one could be more opulent.' He let the audience pass it round, then made sure he got it back. 'Now, what did you notice about it?'

'It's gold and shiny,' one little girl piped up.

He smiled. 'Absolutely right. It's a new one, so my bride's parents will know that I'm wealthy enough to buy her jewellery and I haven't just borrowed it from my mum. Anyone else notice anything?'

'There's a pattern on it,' another child offered.

'That's right.' He smiled at Isobel, then showed the audience the pattern on the front. 'What sort of pattern?'

'Two hands,' one of the children said.

'It's a claddagh ring,' one of the mums offered.

'Not *quite* a claddagh—though that also has two clasped hands, it usually has a heart between them to represent true love, and a crown or fleur-de-lys carved over the top for loyalty,' Alex explained. 'There's a very pretty story behind that—about three hundred years ago, a fisherman from Claddagh in Ireland was captured by Spanish pirates and sold into slavery. His new master taught him how to be a gold-smith, and every day he stole a speck of gold from the floor and after many years he had enough to make a ring to remind him of his sweetheart back in Claddagh. Eventually he escaped and made his way home—to find that his sweetheart was still waiting for him. And he gave her the ring to prove his love.'

Oh, Lord. She could practically see various hearts melting right before him. He definitely had this audience in the palm of his hand. Half the women in the audience were clearly imagining that he was the Irish fisherman about to give her a gold ring.

And Alex was on a roll.

'This is actually a replica of a Roman betrothal ring, and the hand clasped at the wrist represents Concordia, the goddess of agreement,' he said. 'But, as with the claddagh ring, the design also symbolises love and fidelity. It's sometimes called a "fedes" ring.' He smiled. 'Does anyone know why an engagement ring is put on the third finger?'

A chorus of no—and now practically all the women in the audience were gazing longingly at Alex, Isobel noticed. Hardly surprising: in a toga and sandals, he looked fantastic.

He lifted Isobel's left hand and stroked his fingertip along the length of her ring finger. 'The Romans followed the Egyptian belief that there was a vein in this finger that led straight to the heart, so it was important to capture it within a ring—a symbol of unbroken eternity.' He slid the ring onto Isobel's finger. 'Like so.'

A shiver went down her spine. He was acting...wasn't he?

'Aren't you the guy from the telly?' one of the women asked. 'You did that programme on Egypt last year. *The Hunter.*'

'Uh, yes,' Alex said.

'So you work here now?' she asked.

He smiled. 'No. My fiancée does.' He draped one arm around Isobel's shoulders. 'I just hijacked her exhibition. But that's how people got engaged in Roman times—exactly as we got engaged just now.' He took Isobel's left hand and raised it to his lips. 'Sorry about that, Bel. I mean, Flavia.'

'He... I...' Isobel squirmed. 'Sorry, everyone. This wasn't planned. And he isn't supposed to be here.'

'Don't worry, she's not going to get into trouble,' Alex said in a stage whisper. 'I talked to her boss first.'

He'd talked to her boss? What? When?

'Oh, that's so romantic,' another of the women said, sighing. 'To surprise you at work like that.'

'Given what she does for a living, I couldn't really do anything else,' Alex said. 'And if you'll excuse us, Flavia has finished work for today.'

'Alex, I—' she began.

'Shh.' He placed his finger on her lips. 'I cleared it with your boss. Thank you, everyone, for being our witnesses today in a genuine Roman betrothal ceremony.'

Everyone started clapping and calling out their congratulations. Alex smiled back, then simply picked up all the elements of Isobel's display, took her hand, and shepherded her out of the gallery.

'Alex, I can't believe you just did that!' she said in a low voice.

'Stop worrying. I really did clear it with your boss. Rita also let me borrow the outfit—which I need to return, so let's go and change.'

'You borrowed the senator's outfit?'

'I wanted to surprise you,' he said with a grin.

'You did that, all right. I thought you were in the interview this afternoon?'

'I was.'

'And you were going to text me to let me know how it went.'

He shrugged. 'I decided to come and tell you in person.'

'So did you get the job?'

'This morning, you were very confident in my abilities.' He tutted. 'Clearly I'll have to take you home and remind you just how able I am.'

'Alex,' she said warningly, 'if you don't tell me right *now*, I'll stab you with these tweezers. They might be replicas, but they'll hurt.'

He laughed. 'Yes. I got the job. And I'm taking you out to dinner to celebrate—that, and our engagement.'

'Our engagement?' She glanced at the ring. 'I thought you were…I dunno…hamming it up.'

'No. You just got engaged to me, Bel. In public, so you can't back out—and, besides, we're meant to be seeing the parents at the weekend. They're expecting to see a ring.' His eyes glittered. 'Do you like it?'

'It's gorgeous. And it's a perfect fit—but how did you know my size?'

'Give me some credit for resourcefulness.'

'No, I want to know.'

'While you were in the shower a few days ago, I borrowed one of your rings and drew round it. I took the drawing to the jeweller's and asked them to size it for me—and I gave them a photograph of exactly what I wanted them to make for me. I picked it up on the way here. It's eighteen-carat so it's more durable.' He paused. 'I know it's not exactly a modern engagement ring, but I thought this was more you.' He smiled at her. 'Though if you want a diamond, that's fine—we can go shopping for one whenever you like.'

'No. This is perfect.' She shook her head. 'I can't quite

believe this just happened. You borrowed the senator's robes and hijacked my show—'

'With factually correct information,' he cut in.

'Skimpy, but I suppose it'll do.'

'Skimpy?' He scoffed, then bent his head to whisper in her ear, 'But, seeing as you brought it up…skimpy can be good. Are you dressed *completely* as a Roman woman?'

'What do you mean?'

'Because, if you are, then I know you're not wearing very much underneath that robe. And in that case I sincerely hope your office has a blind at the window and a lock on the door.'

'It's open plan.'

'Pity.' He nibbled her ear lobe. 'Looks as if we'll have to go home before dinner…'

CHAPTER SIX

WHEN Isobel walked into the office, she was surprised to see a large card propped up in the middle of her desk along with a beautiful bouquet of flowers; the card attached to the flowers made tears well up in her eyes when she read it. *'Isobel and Alex. Congratulations and much love.'* It was from the whole department—and they could only have known about this a few minutes ago. Someone must have organised a collection at record speed and gone straight out to buy the flowers even as Alex had been striding towards her in his toga.

'Congratulations, Bel.' Rita, Isobel's boss, came over to her and hugged her. 'I'm so pleased for you, love.'

'Though you kept it very quiet,' Siobhan, the department secretary, said. 'I thought you two were just good friends?'

'Not any more,' Alex said, smiling back at her and draping his arm round Isobel's shoulders.

'Let's see the ring.' Rita looked at it, then nodded her approval at Alex. 'It's lovely. And very much our Isobel.' She smiled at Isobel again. 'And don't you dare sneak off and get married in secret, do you hear?'

'We won't,' Alex promised with a smile. 'In fact, I want to have a chat with you about that.'

Isobel could guess exactly where this was heading. 'No,

Alex, we're not having a Roman wedding in the middle of the Roman gallery. Apart from the fact it's not licensed for weddings... *No.*'

'Spoilsport,' Alex grumbled, but he was laughing. 'Rita, I know it's a bit of a cheek, but would you mind if I sweep my new fiancée off for dinner right now rather than waiting until the end of her shift? We've got a few things to celebrate.'

Rita smiled broadly. 'It's not every day someone gets engaged around here. Of course I don't mind. Shoo. Go and have fun.'

'I'll stay late tomorrow night to make up the time,' Isobel offered.

'No need, love. Apart from the fact that you already put in more hours than you should, I believe a happy staff is a productive staff.' Rita smiled. 'Though you two *might* want to change back into normal clothes before you leave the building.'

'We'd turn a few heads, dressed like this,' Alex agreed, laughing.

By the time Isobel had changed, Alex had ordered a taxi, which was waiting outside for them.

'That's so *extravagant*,' she said.

'It's also much easier than carrying a bouquet on the tube in the rush hour,' he pointed out as he opened the taxi door for her, then placed the flowers on her lap before climbing in beside her.

'I can't believe they managed to do all this between you asking Rita if you could hijack my display, and you taking me back to my office.'

'Everyone likes you, Bel,' he said simply. 'Of course they'd want to do something for you—and not wait until tomorrow, either.'

She opened the card. 'Everyone in the department's signed

the card. Look at all these messages wishing us luck and so much happiness together.' She blinked back the threatening tears. 'This is all wrong. I feel such a fake, Alex.'

'You're not a fake. And it's not wrong. We've been through this, Bel. This marriage is going to work, because we're very, very good friends.' He moved slightly closer, and whispered, 'Plus we're having great sex. Which in my book is a million times better than falling in love and being as miserable as hell.'

She frowned. 'What happened, Alex? Who was she?'

'Who?'

'The woman who made you so bitter about love.'

He shrugged. 'It was a long time ago.'

'She must've hurt you a lot,' Isobel said softly, curling her fingers round his, 'for you to avoid a relationship for all these years.' She couldn't even remember him bringing anyone back to meet his parents.

'As I said, it was a long time ago.'

'And if you're still hurting…'

'I'm not. I'm over it.' Alex sighed. 'All right. If you have to know the gory details, I was working on my PhD. I was on a dig down on the south coast, and Dorinda lived in the next village. Like most of the locals, she'd come to take a look at what we were doing at the dig. She was the most beautiful woman I'd ever seen—glamorous, with all that long dark hair and legs that went on for ever.'

So that was why he always dated stick-insect brunettes. Because he was looking for another Dorinda. Right at that moment, Isobel wished she'd never asked.

But Alex was still talking.

'I was a geeky student who still practically had teenage spots, and I thought she was way out of my reach. But then I found out that she liked me, too.'

Geeky?

Alex had never been geeky, as far as she could remember. Or covered in spots.

'We had a drink together, and it snowballed from there into a mad summer affair. I spent every second with her I could. And, yeah, a lot of it was in bed.' His expression turned grim. 'She told me she was divorced, or I would never have started seeing her.'

Isobel believed him. Alex had a strong code of honour.

'I was actually planning to ask her to marry me. I hadn't got as far as choosing a ring and working out a romantic place to propose, but I was close to it. But then her husband came back. It turned out I was just a diversion because she was bored.' His smile was tinged with bitterness. 'I was twenty-two, remember. Still didn't have a clue how the world worked. And would you believe I was actually stupid enough to say to her that I'd thought she loved me? She just laughed and asked me why on earth she'd want to go off with a student who had no money and no prospects of having any, when her husband was practically a millionaire.'

'Sounds as if you had a lucky escape.' She tightened her fingers round his again. 'Alex, she wasn't worth it. And if you've been hurting all these years over her...'

'I haven't been brooding on it, exactly. But it left a nasty taste in my mouth.' He grimaced. 'She'd cheated on her husband with me. She'd lied to us both, played us both for a fool. And I hated the fact that she'd used me to hurt someone else.'

'Not everyone's like that.'

'I know. But her husband was away for long periods—just like I was. So it made me stop and think. Supposing I'd got married and left my wife on her own all the time...'

'Your wife wouldn't necessarily have cheated on you.'

'Maybe not *intentionally*, Bel. But these things happen. With me being away so much, she would've been lonely. Vulnerable. An easy target for anyone who showed her the affection she wasn't getting from me because I wasn't there. And I didn't want to take that kind of risk. It was easier to stay single and keep my relationships short and sweet—and to focus on my job.'

'You're still going to be away a lot with this job. So do you think I'm going to be unfaithful to you?' she asked.

'Of course I don't.' His eyes glittered. 'Apart from the fact that you're not a liar or a cheat, we're not going into this all hormonally charged and with rose-coloured glasses on and declaring all the hearts and flowers stuff. And I hope you know that I won't be unfaithful to you, either.'

'This feels more like a business arrangement than a marriage.'

'It's not a business arrangement. It's a sensible arrangement,' Alex said as the taxi pulled up outside her flat. 'And you and I will never lie to each other, so it's going to work out just fine.'

Guilt flooded through her. Lies didn't have to be direct; lies could also be caused by omission. And she was keeping something important from him.

She really had to tell him.

Soon.

He paid the driver, then let them in—almost, she thought, as if he'd lived there for ever and wasn't just using her spare set of keys. 'I need to get changed,' he said.

'You look good in a suit.'

'But I hate wearing it. It makes me feel...' he clenched his fists and paced up and down the room '..."cabin'd, cribb'd, confin'd."'

'Ooh, get the drama king,' she teased. 'Though you're more of an Antony than a Macbeth.'

'What, an ageing roué whose brains are in his trousers?' He pulled a face. 'Which makes you a middle-aged tart who doesn't have the courage of her convictions—and takes a whole act to die, while talking about making the briefest end.'

'Oi! I *like* that play,' she protested.

He smiled. 'Next time it's on at the Globe, we'll go. But before you dive for the what's on listings, I really need to wash my hair.'

She laughed. 'You're being prissy about your hair? Don't tell me you're planning to get a haircut, now you're officially a consultant.'

'Am I, hell,' he scoffed. 'My hair's fine as it is. Well, when it's not oiled back so I can fake a Roman haircut.' He raised an eyebrow. 'Hey, you didn't happen to bring that strigil home from your Roman beauty kit, did you?'

'No,' she said, guessing what he had in mind, 'and I'm sure you wouldn't like traditional Roman hygiene.'

'I dunno.' His eyes glittered. 'I quite like the idea of sauntering into a caldarium and having you scrape me off with a strigil.'

She laughed. 'Alex. You're impossible.'

'Who, me?' he deadpanned. 'Look, I don't want to get olive oil all over this suit, so would you mind giving me a hand undressing?'

'That has to be the most trumped-up excuse I've ever heard.'

'I thought it was quite a good one, actually.' He gave her a wicked smile. 'Come and have a shower with me.'

'Now there's an offer,' she said, rolling her eyes. But she slid his jacket from his shoulders and hung it over the back of a chair. He hadn't put his tie back on when he'd changed out of the toga, and he looked incredibly sexy in dark trousers and a white shirt with the top button undone.

She unbuttoned his shirt, and ran her hands lightly over his chest. 'Mmm. The barbarian look. I like it.'

KATE HARDY   77

'Do you, now?' Alex's response was to make short work of her clothes and the remainder of his own; then he picked her up and carried her into the bathroom.

Isobel laughed. 'You really are a barbarian, Alex.'

'Just living up to your view of me.' He set her on her feet in the bath, stepped in next to her, and switched the water on.

Isobel shrieked. 'That's cold!'

'Don't be a baby.' He grabbed the shower gel. 'All righty— you're Flavia the patrician matron and I'm your barbarian slave.'

She laughed. 'Shouldn't you have scented oil and a strigil if you're my barbarian slave?'

'This is much more civilised,' he said loftily.

'You? Civilised?'

'I can be.' He gave her a lascivious wink, then poured shower gel into his palms, lathered it, and glided his fingers over her skin. 'Mmm. Bel. Your skin feels nice. Turn round.'

She did so, and he lathered her shoulders and her back, then drew her back against his body. She could feel his erection pressing against her; then he fanned his fingers across her abdomen and then stroked gently upwards until he could cup her breasts.

'Better still,' he whispered, kissing the curve of her neck as his thumbs and forefingers played with her nipples.

She wriggled against him. 'Barbarian.'

He nibbled her earlobe. 'At your command, my lady.'

She turned round again to face him. 'I don't think you'd be at anyone's command except your own, Alex.'

He kissed her lightly. 'You could command me to make love with you. I'd obey you.'

She slid her fingers down to grasp his erection. 'Only because it's what you want to do.'

'It's a win-win situation, Bel. Apart from the fact that

you've turned round, which means we switch roles,' he added with a grin.

'We do?'

'Uh-huh. You have to obey me, because I'm the patrician now.'

She gave him a wicked grin. 'But you look like a barbarian. I'll just get the tweezers to sort you out, my Lord.'

'Don't you dare.' He lifted her up and pinned her against the tiles.

She yelped. 'Alex, that's *freezing*!'

'I'll warm you up, then.' He kissed her hard, his mouth urgent against hers. Her hands were locked round his neck, holding him close, and he'd moved so he could push one hand between her thighs, stroking her and teasing her until she was quivering.

'Now?' he asked softly.

'N-now.' She could barely speak, she was so turned on.

He lifted her slightly so he could fit the tip of his penis against the entrance of her sex, then slowly pushed into her.

'Alex,' she whispered, and jammed her mouth over his.

The water was pouring over them and Isobel was so aware of every single movement Alex made—the slow, deliberate thrusts as he brought her nearer and nearer to the edge, the way his body fitted hers perfectly—and she knew the exact second his self-control snapped and his body surged into hers. Although her eyes were tightly closed, she could see starbursts; and all she could do was hold on tightly to Alex as her climax rocked through her.

Finally, he eased out of her and set her on her feet. 'Um. When did the hot water run out?'

'No idea,' she said.

'Sorry.'

And he really did look contrite. She smiled. 'I'm not.' She

reached up and touched his hair. 'Except for this. You still need to get rid of that olive oil. I'll go and boil the kettle so you've got some hot water to do your hair.'

'Thanks. I wouldn't want to look a total scruff when I take you out to dinner.'

She raised an eyebrow. 'Are you telling me you're going to wear your suit again tonight?'

'No. Suits are overrated.' He kissed her again. 'I'm not wearing a tie, either.'

But by the time she'd dried her hair and he'd dressed, she had to admit he looked good. Black trousers and a turquoise silk shirt that, on Alex, just heightened his raw masculinity.

'You scrub up rather nicely—for a barbarian.'

'Watch it, or the hat goes on,' he teased back. 'Come on, beautiful. Let's go celebrate my new job—and our engagement.'

The endearment warmed her. Alex thought her beautiful?

Probably just a figure of speech.

But she was glad he'd made the effort.

And she was starting to believe that he was right. This was going to work out just fine.

CHAPTER SEVEN

On Sunday, Alex drove Isobel to the little market town in the Cotswolds where they'd grown up. They'd arranged to meet their parents at the local hotel, along with Alex's sister Saskia and her husband Bryn and baby Flora. Alex's twin sisters, Helen and Polly, were both away for the weekend, but he'd said wryly that their parents wouldn't wait any longer for them to turn up as an engaged couple—if they didn't go to the Cotswolds, their families would come straight to London and besiege the flat.

The second they walked into the dining room, their respective mothers spotted them and started waving. And it was a good ten minutes before the hugs and the congratulations and the official inspection of the engagement ring were over.

'What a welcome,' Isobel said, smiling as she sat down.

'Well, of course! This is a celebration. It's not every day my daughter gets engaged.' Stuart made what was clearly a pre-arranged signal to the waiter, who immediately brought over champagne.

'Getting engaged to the boy next door after all these years. It's so *romantic*,' Marcia said, smiling at them.

Saskia rolled her eyes. 'This is Alex we're talking about, Mum. Your son doesn't do romance.'

'Of course I do,' Alex protested.

No, he didn't, Isobel thought. But they were meant to be putting on a show for their parents, so she didn't correct him.

He nudged her. 'Bel, tell them how we got engaged.'

She smiled. 'He hijacked my talk on Roman beauty—came strutting up in a toga, told everyone all about betrothal customs, and then put the ring on my finger.'

'You got engaged in the *museum*?' Anna asked.

'It was romantic,' Alex protested.

'That's so you, Alex,' Marcia said ruefully.

'And so Isobel, too,' Anna added, laughing. 'You've got a rival for my daughter's affections in her job, you know, Alex.'

He laughed. 'You could say the same about me. But we'll put each other first, won't we, Bel?'

'Of course,' she chipped in.

'So you bought her a Roman betrothal ring and you had a Roman engagement.' Saskia raised an eyebrow. 'Does this mean you're going to have a Roman wedding, too?'

Isobel groaned. 'Don't encourage him, Saskia.'

'No. It'll be an ordinary civil wedding,' Alex said. 'Close family only. As in you lot plus Helen and Polly and their husbands and the boys.'

'Well, congratulations,' Stuart said, raising his glass. 'And welcome to the family, Alex.'

'Thank you,' Alex said, smiling.

'Welcome to the family, Bel,' Tom echoed, raising his own glass. 'We've always thought of you as family anyway, but it's good to make you officially one of us.'

Isobel swallowed the lump in her throat. 'Thank you. I think I'm going to cry.'

'No, you're not.' Alex, who'd made sure he was sitting next to her, scooped her onto his lap and wrapped his arms round her waist, holding her close.

'So have you set a date or anything?' Saskia asked.

'No,' Alex admitted, 'but as we've known each other for years, there's not much point in having a long engagement. As it's a small wedding, it won't take long to organise—so are you all busy in three weeks' time?'

Isobel almost choked on her champagne. 'Alex, I can't possibly organise a wedding in three weeks!'

'But I can,' he said. 'I'm twiddling my thumbs for the next month until I start my new job. Three weeks to the wedding, a week's honeymoon—and this will give me something to do in the meantime and keep me out of mischief.' He smiled. 'Actually, it'll be fun.'

'Why does that set all the alarm bells ringing in the back of my head?' Isobel asked.

'Because you know what my brother's like,' Saskia said. 'He could be planning anything.'

'Alex, maybe we'd better wait until you've been in your job for a few months,' Isobel suggested. And it would buy her some time, too. So she could find the right moment to tell him about what had happened with Gary. Explain about the miscarriages. She was marrying him under false pretences as it was. She couldn't do it under double false pretences.

'No, he's got a point,' Anna said, surprising Isobel. 'You've known each other for years. Why wait? And a summer wedding will be lovely.'

'I think so, too,' Marcia said. 'Don't worry that he's going to go over the top, Bel. We'll keep him under control—won't we, Anna?'

'Absolutely,' Anna said. 'I foresee daily phone calls and updates.'

'I'll text you,' Alex said, laughing at the horrified look on his mother's face.

Saskia dug him in the ribs. 'Don't be mean. You know

Mum hardly ever switches her mobile phone on and gets in a knot over texting.'

'All right, all right. Daily updates. In a phone call,' Alex promised.

'I think we need a toast,' Marcia said, beaming. 'To Isobel and Alex. And may they have a very long, very happy married life.'

'Isobel and Alex,' everyone echoed.

Alex bent his head to whisper in Isobel's ear, 'Stop worrying. It's all going to be fine.'

'No snogging at the table, you two,' Saskia directed. 'Let the poor girl go back to her seat, Alex. It's lunchtime. Flora's been really patient but if we don't feed her in the next ten seconds she's going to start screaming.'

'Just like her mother,' Bryn said.

Alex laughed. 'You can say that again.' He lifted Isobel's hand, kissed her palm and folded her fingers over the place he'd just kissed. 'As my little sister's being bossy...'

'Yes, dear.' Isobel fluttered her eyelashes at him, laughed and slid off his lap to reclaim her seat.

It was the perfect lunch. Everyone was laughing and talking and smiling, and Isobel's heart gave a funny little throb as she thought how much she loved all the people there.

Including Alex.

But Alex didn't feel the same way about her. If she wasn't very, very careful, she was going to get her heart broken all over again. And this time she wouldn't be able to put the pieces back together.

Isobel was really quiet on the way home, Alex noticed.

'Are you all right?' he asked.

'Yes, of course.'

But her smile was fixed rather than genuine. He reached

across to take her hand and squeeze it. 'No, you're not. What is it? The wedding?'

She sighed. 'Yes.'

'Going to tell me about it?'

'I've been married before,' she said softly. 'I've done the church and the partying and it all went wrong.'

'Because you trusted in love,' he said. 'This time, we're going for something that lasts—we like each other and we get on well, so it'll work. And I can guarantee this wedding's not going to be anything like your first one.' He slid her a wicked look. 'For a start, the groom will be wearing an Akubra.'

'You're *kidding!*'

Oh, he loved this. She was so easy to tease. 'You don't want me to wear my Hunter stuff? OK. We'll make it a Roman do and I'll sweet-talk Rita into lending me that toga again.'

'Alex…'

He could hear in her voice that he'd just pushed her over the edge into worrying again. 'I was teasing, Bel. As our mothers are both keeping an eye on me, I can't do anything too outrageous, can I?'

'I suppose not,' she admitted. 'Though I'd be happier if you actually planned it with me.'

'Bel, you're up to your eyes at work. The last thing you need when you get home is to have to go through all the hassle of choosing this and booking that and seeing if there's an alternative if we can't have our first choice.' He rubbed the pad of his thumb across the backs of her fingers. 'Whereas I'm not officially at work for another month. I don't have anything pressing to do, so it makes sense for me to be the one making the arrangements and chasing things up. And, actually, I'd get a huge kick out of giving you a surprise wedding. A day to remember for all the right reasons.'

She swallowed hard. 'Alex, I really need to talk to you about something.'

'Bel, it's going to be fine,' he said softly. 'I'm not going to plan anything you'll hate. Just trust me.'

'I do trust you. It's not that. It's…' She sighed. 'Now isn't the right place. But there's something you ought to know. About me.'

'Your divorce never came through properly?'

She shook her head. 'No, that's sorted. Gary made sure of that when his—' for a moment, her voice cracked '—when his partner became pregnant.'

'So there's no legal bar to us getting married. Good. So do you want a church wedding or a civil wedding?'

'I'm divorced,' she reminded him. 'I can't marry in church.'

'You could still have a blessing, if you want one.'

'Civil's fine. And something quiet, Alex. Not a media circus.'

'It won't be a media circus,' he promised. 'So the mums and Saskia are coming to help you find a wedding dress, next weekend?'

'Yes.' She dragged in a breath. 'But this is all happening so fast.'

'Relax. We have three weeks. And whatever I say about loathing admin, I'm actually quite good at organising things. I'm not going to skimp any of the little details—or anything major, come to that.' He gave her a sidelong look. 'So I take it you're not going for the meringue dress?'

'Been there, done that.'

'That's a no, then.' He paused. 'Tell you what would look good. A little shift dress—you know, like the one Audrey Hepburn wears in *Breakfast at Tiffany's*.'

'A *black* wedding dress?'

'No.' He rolled his eyes. 'I was talking shape, not colour. White would be good, because it would go with your flame-coloured veil.'

'What flame-coloured…?' She groaned. 'Oh, no. Saskia put the idea in your head. We're not having a Roman wedding and I'm *not* wearing a flame-coloured veil.'

He pursed his lips. 'It'd look stunning in the photographs.'

'Alex!'

He laughed. 'All right, all right. I'll leave the dress up to you. But just remember the mums and my sister will all be sworn to absolute secrecy about the finer details, so when you go shopping there's no point in even asking them what I'm planning.'

'You're impossible.'

'If what I have in mind is doable, you're going to enjoy it, I promise you that much.'

She was silent for a while, and he was aware of her fidgeting next to him.

'All right. What now?'

'Nothing.'

He sighed. 'Bel, don't pull that girly stuff on me. What's the matter?'

'Are you at least going to tell me where we're going on holiday?'

He noted her choice of word: holiday, not honeymoon. Good. So she wasn't about to go sentimental on him. 'Nope.'

'So how do I know what to pack? Or if I need any vaccinations?'

'You don't need any vaccinations—and we're not going anywhere that involves mosquitoes or even the tiniest possibility of malaria. As for packing…wear what you want.'

She sighed. 'Will you at least tell me if it's going to be cold or hot?'

'Better than that. I'll pack for you.'

She growled in frustration. 'I hate you.'

'No, you don't. Just humour me, Bel. I want to do something nice for you—and I like giving surprises.'

'I don't like receiving surprises.'

'Because you're a control freak,' he teased.

'I'm not. You're a steamroller.'

'Insulting me isn't going to make any difference. I'm still not going to tell you anything.' He chuckled. 'Though you could try seducing it out of me.'

'Maybe I'll do a Lysistrata on you,' she fenced.

He got the reference to the ancient Greek play immediately. 'Go on a sex strike? You can try, honey.' His luck was in, because there was a lay-by ahead. He signalled, parked the car, then removed his seat belt. 'But that's not going to work.'

'Oh, really?' She lifted her chin at the challenge.

'Really. Let me show you why.' He undid her seat belt, yanked her into his arms, and kissed her. Teasing, nibbling kisses along her lower lip until she gave in and opened her mouth, letting him deepen the kiss. He slid one hand underneath her top, stroking her skin in the way he knew she liked; she slid her arms round his neck and drew him closer.

He moved one hand up to cup her breast, rubbing the pad of his thumb against her hardening nipple through the lace of her bra, then broke the kiss.

'That,' he said softly, 'is why a sex strike wouldn't work. Because it's good between us, and your body knows it. Right now, your nipples are hard, just as right now I'm hard for you and I really, really want to be inside you.'

Her cheeks flamed. 'So you're saying I'm easy?'

'No. Just that it's good between us.' He stroked her face. 'And if it makes you feel any better, I'm not going to be very comfortable while I'm driving us home. Right now, I can't think of anything I'd like more than to carry you out of the car, lay you down on the nice soft grass and wrap your legs round my waist.'

She shivered, and he knew she wanted it, too.

'But as having sex in public could get us arrested, I'll go for option two.'

'Which is?'

'To drive home as fast as possible without getting a speeding fine. And then I'm going to take all your clothes off. And then…' He gave her a wicked grin. 'Then I'm going to make you beg.'

She scoffed. 'In your dreams, big boy.'

He kissed her again. 'No, honey. In ours.'

CHAPTER EIGHT

THE next week simply flew by. Isobel was really busy at work; so she had to admit that no way would she have had the time to organise the wedding herself, or even help Alex much.

But by Friday night she knew she had to talk to him. Before she went shopping for a wedding dress. Before things went too far. Because once he knew the truth, he might change his mind about getting married.

As she walked up the steps to her flat, her feet felt like lead. This was a conversation she really didn't want to have. But if she didn't speak up now and things went pear-shaped in the future, Alex would never forgive her for lying to him.

One of the reasons he'd reacted so badly to Dorinda's betrayal was that she'd lied and cheated.

Right now, she was no better. She could be cheating him out of a future.

And hadn't Alex himself said that their marriage would work because they'd never lie to each other?

When she reached the front door, she dragged in a breath. Nerved herself. And walked indoors to face Alex.

'Hi.' He looked up from his laptop and smiled at her. 'How was your day?'

'Fine.' Lord, how she wanted to back out of this right now. To pretend that nothing was wrong. But she couldn't do that to him. 'Alex, we need to talk. I need to tell you something.' Forestalling his interruption, she held up a hand. 'There's no easy way to say it, so I'm going to just come out with it. And I don't want you saying a word until I've finished, OK?'

He frowned, but nodded. 'Hit me with it.'

'It's why Gary and I split up. And I'll understand if you want to walk away now.' She closed her eyes, unable to bear looking at him and seeing the pity in his face. 'We…we tried to start a family. Except I lost the baby. Both times. And…' she gulped '…you said you maybe wanted a family. I might not be able to give you that.'

He was silent.

Just as she'd expected.

And now he was going to walk away. Just as Gary had.

She dragged in a breath, still with her eyes closed—and the next thing she knew, she was in Alex's arms and he was holding her really, really tightly.

'Alex? What…?'

'I agreed not to say a word until you'd finished,' he reminded her.

'I—I've f-finished now.' To her horror, her voice was actually wobbly.

'Oh, Bel. I had no idea you'd been through something like this. I'm so sorry.'

Sorry, because he didn't want to marry her any more?

But then why were his arms still round her? Why was he still holding her close to him, as if she were the most precious thing in the world? This was Alex—the man who didn't even believe in love.

'I'm sorry,' he said softly, 'that you had to go through something so heartbreaking. I just assumed that he wanted kids and you didn't, because you've always been so dedicated to your job.'

She swallowed hard. 'I wanted a baby. I wanted a baby so *much*, Alex. And when Gary and I couldn't…' She closed her eyes again. 'When he left me, I thought I'd never have another chance to have a child of my own. I've tried so hard to suppress it—so hard to make my job, my life, be enough for me. And it's got worse since Saskia had Flora. Every time I hold my god-daughter…' The wave of longing was so strong, she could hardly breathe. 'I never thought I'd be the broody type, but it doesn't seem I have a choice in the matter. It's her weight, the perfect size to cradle in my arms, her warmth, that new baby smell. Everything.'

'So what happened? Did the doctors say why you miscarried?'

'Just that it's really common before twelve weeks. It happens to lots and lots of women.'

'Did they do any tests?'

The question hurt, but his voice was so gentle. No judgement. No blame. 'They don't even consider looking into the causes until you've had at least three miscarriages.' And that was the worst part. She tried to swallow the tears. 'Gary didn't want to take the chance of losing a third baby. And I guess I was a becoming a bit difficult to live with.'

'What?' Alex shook his head, as if trying to clear it. 'Are you telling me he walked out on you, and said it was *your* fault?'

'I…' She let her head rest against his shoulder. 'Yes,' she admitted brokenly.

'Right at this moment, I'd like to break every bone on his body, then peg him out in the desert in Turkey, smear him in honey and leave him to the ants.'

Isobel pulled back and stared at Alex in shock. She'd

never, ever heard him sound angry like this before. Coldly, *viciously* angry.

'But that's not going to change the past—or the fact he hurt you. That he let you down when you needed him.' Still keeping one arm wrapped round her, he stroked her cheek. 'Here's what we're going to do. You want a baby.'

She dragged in a breath. 'Yes.'

'You helped me get what I want, Bel, so I'm going to do the same for you. After we get married, we're going to try for a baby.'

'But what if…?' She couldn't bring herself to ask the rest of the question.

But he seemed to guess what she couldn't say. 'We'll see how things go. And if it doesn't work out, we'll talk to the doctors. Get tests. Find out what the problem is and see what our options are.'

She swallowed hard. '*I'm* the problem.'

'And how do you work that out?'

'Gary has a baby now. So it can't be him, can it?'

Alex smoothed the hair off her face. 'I'm not a medic and I don't know anywhere near enough about miscarriages to give an informed opinion. But things are never that clear-cut, Bel. Don't blame yourself.'

She made a noncommittal murmur.

'Seriously, Bel. Don't blame yourself.' He paused. 'When you told me about Gary's new partner and the baby, I thought you were upset because you were still in love with him.'

She shook her head. 'My love for him died a long time ago. I don't envy her because she has him. It's because…' Because of the baby. The baby she'd wanted so much herself. She paused. 'Look, I understand if you want to call the wedding off.'

His eyes glittered. 'Two weeks tomorrow, Isobel Martin,

we're getting married. And we're going on honeymoon. And we're going to make a family of our own.'

The tears she'd been trying so hard to hold back were suddenly too much for her. She could feel her eyes brimming, feel the wetness leaking down her face even though she tried to stop it.

With the pad of his thumb, Alex wiped the tears away. 'This doesn't change anything about our marriage, Bel. It just proves I'm right about love. It lets you down.' He dipped his head to kiss her very lightly on the mouth. Gentle and un-threatening. 'But I'm not going to let you down. That's a promise.'

And Alex was the kind of man who always kept his promises.

'Come on. Give me a smile,' he coaxed.

She tried. And failed.

He rubbed the tip of his nose against hers. 'I think you need food. Though I can't cook because there's nothing in the fridge. I'd planned to take you out to dinner, tonight.'

'Alex, that's lovely of you, but I'm really not hungry.' Right then she felt as if food would choke her. And after baring her soul to Alex, she felt too raw, too exposed even to go out of the flat.

He stroked her cheek. 'OK. I understand. So let's stay in.' He stroked her hair. 'What I want to do right now is hold you close—just you and me, skin to skin. I'm not going to lie to you, Bel. I can't promise that I'm going to make everything all right for you—but I can promise that I'm going to try my hardest.'

She let him draw her to her feet. Let him strip away her clothes, the way she'd stripped away her emotional barriers. He just held her in silence for a while, his arms wrapped pro-tectively round her. And when they made love, later that night,

Alex was so tender, so cherishing, that just for a while she allowed herself to believe that he felt the same way about her as she was beginning to feel about him. And maybe, just maybe, her dreams were going to come true.

The following morning, Isobel woke to an empty space beside her. Judging by how cold the sheets were, Alex had been gone for a while.

She pulled on a dressing gown and padded into the living room. Alex was curled up on the sofa, working on his laptop and nursing a mug of coffee. He looked up when she walked in and quickly saved whatever file he was working on. 'Morning, Bel. I was going to wake you in about half an hour.'

'It's Saturday. How come you're up so early?' Because he'd had time to think about what she'd told him last night, and changed his mind?

'I'm always awake early.' He shrugged. 'And you needed some sleep. I thought I'd work out here so I didn't disturb you.' There was a distinct twinkle in his eye. 'Besides, I can hardly give you a surprise wedding day if you're able to look over my shoulder and see what I'm doing.'

The knot of tension between her shoulders loosened slightly. 'What's to stop me doing that now?'

'I've closed the file. And the whole lot's password-protected, so it's pointless you even *trying* to open it.'

'I could,' she said, pursing her lips, 'hack my way in. I have friends who are good with computers and they'll tell me how to do it if I ask them nicely.'

He laughed. 'But you're not going to, or I'll tell the mums and they'll nag you stupid. What time are they getting here?'

'They're not. I'm meeting them at the train station.' She glanced at the clock on the mantelpiece. 'Oh, help. I didn't realise it was that late!' She frowned. 'But my alarm didn't go off.' She hadn't bothered looking at the clock before she got out of bed, assuming that she'd woken before her alarm went off.

'I turned it off,' he admitted, 'because I thought you could do with some sleep.'

'I'm going to be late now, and they'll worry.'

'They won't. Go have your shower and I'll text Mum to let her know.'

'Alex, she never picks up texts. Better ring her or text Saskia instead,' Isobel called from the bathroom door.

It was the quickest shower on record and for once she didn't bother washing her hair. But by the time she was ready, Alex had a cup of coffee waiting for her. 'I added enough cold water so you can drink it straight down,' he said. When she'd done so, he handed her an apple and a banana. 'Breakfast to go.'

'Is this what you do when you're on a project?'

He grinned. 'Hey, it's healthy. At least I wasn't suggesting what some of my colleagues used to do—doughnuts and coffee with four sugars. Carb overload.' He kissed her lightly. 'See you when you get back. Have a good time.'

'Thanks, Alex. And, um, about last night…' She swallowed hard. 'I wanted to say thank you. For understanding.'

He laid his palm against her cheek. 'Stop worrying. This is me you're talking to. There are no pedestals for either of us to fall off. Go and find yourself a nice frock.' His lips twitched. 'And a flame-coloured veil.'

Isobel met their mothers and Saskia as planned at the railway station, albeit slightly late. And although she tried to get some information out of them about the wedding, none of them would tell her a single thing about Alex's plans.

'He'd have our guts for garters,' Marcia said. 'No can do.'

'But I promise you'll love it,' Saskia added.

Anna nodded agreement. 'And I know now just how much Alex loves you—because he's gone to a lot of trouble to make it the perfect day.'

He didn't love her, Isobel thought. Not in the way her mother believed he did. But that was something she didn't want to explain, so she allowed herself to be distracted by dresses.

'This,' Anna said, holding out a cream silk shift dress, 'is perfect.' She made Isobel try it on and come and pirouette for the three of them. 'That's the one,' she said.

Meanwhile, Marcia found the perfect pair of high-heeled cream court shoes to go with the dress. And they had them in Isobel's size.

'That's the difficult bit done, then.' Saskia smiled. 'And I need a coffee break after all that hard work.'

Next were the dresses for the mums. And after the fourth shop, Isobel rubbed the base of her spine. 'Time out. We've been walking for ages. Coffee.'

Marcia looked at her and then at Saskia. 'I've known you two all your lives—and I know full well you can shop all day without a break. Are you doing this because of me?'

'Of course not,' Isobel fibbed, but she couldn't look Marcia in the eye.

'You arranged this between you,' Marcia said suspiciously. 'Breaks practically on the hour. Look, I'm fine. I'm not ill.'

Isobel exchanged a look with her best friend. 'OK. I admit it. We're worried about you, Marcia. You're not an invalid, but you've had a rough time with your health. We don't want to push you too hard.'

'You want to stay well for the wedding, don't you?' Saskia added.

Marcia scowled. 'That's emotional blackmail.'

The Harlequin Reader Service — Here's how it works:

Accepting your 2 free books and 2 free mystery gifts places you under no obligation to buy anything. You may keep the books and gifts and return the shipping statement marked "cancel". If you do not cancel, about a month later we'll send you 6 additional books and bill you just $4.05 each in the U.S. or $4.74 each in Canada. That is a savings of at least 15% off the cover price. It's quite a bargain! Shipping and handling is just 25¢ per book, along with any applicable taxes.* You may cancel at any time, but if you choose to continue, every month we'll send you 6 more books, which you may either purchase at the discount price or return to us and cancel your subscription.

*Terms and prices subject to change without notice. Sales tax applicable in N.Y. Canadian residents will be charged applicable provincial taxes and GST. Offer not valid in Quebec. All orders subject to approval. Credit or debit balances in a customer's account(s) may be offset by any other outstanding balance owed by or to the customer. Please allow 4 to 6 weeks for delivery. Offer available while quantities last.

If offer card is missing write to: The Harlequin Reader Service, 3010 Walden Ave., P.O. Box 1867, Buffalo, NY 14240-1867

NO POSTAGE
NECESSARY
IF MAILED
IN THE
UNITED STATES

BUSINESS REPLY MAIL

FIRST-CLASS MAIL   PERMIT NO. 717   BUFFALO, NY

POSTAGE WILL BE PAID BY ADDRESSEE

HARLEQUIN READER SERVICE
3010 WALDEN AVE
PO BOX 1867
BUFFALO NY 14240-9952

Do You Have the LUCKY KEY?

Scratch the gold areas with a coin. Then check below to see the books and gifts you can get!

PLAY THE Lucky Key Game

and you can get

FREE BOOKS and FREE GIFTS!

YES! I have scratched off the gold areas. Please send me the 2 FREE BOOKS and 2 FREE GIFTS, worth about $10, for which I qualify. I understand I am under no obligation to purchase any books, as explained on the back of this card.

306 HDL EVJ5   **106 HDL EVNH**

FIRST NAME   LAST NAME

ADDRESS

APT.#   CITY

STATE/PROV.   ZIP/POSTAL CODE

www.eHarlequin.com

🔑🔑🔑🔑 2 free books plus 2 free gifts   🔑🔑🔑🔑 1 free book

🔑🔑🔑🔑 2 free books   🔑🔑🔑🔑 Try Again!

Offer limited to one per household and not valid to current subscribers of Harlequin Presents® books.
Your Privacy – Harlequin Books is committed to protecting your privacy. Our Privacy Policy is available online at www.eHarlequin.com or upon request from the Harlequin Reader Service. From time to time we make our lists of customers available to reputable third parties who may have a product or service of interest to you. If you would prefer for us not to share your name and address, please check here. ☐

DETACH AND MAIL CARD TODAY!

(H-P-01/09)

© 2008 HARLEQUIN ENTERPRISES LIMITED ® and ™ are trademarks owned and used by the trademark owner and/or its licensee

'But they're right,' Anna cut in gently. 'They're worried about you, Marcia.' She smiled. 'And I'm ten years older than you, so I vote for a rest, too.'

'I give in,' Marcia said ruefully.

'So are you going to humour Alex about the flame-coloured veil?' Saskia asked over coffee.

'So he *is* planning a Roman wedding,' Isobel said.

'No, no, no, no, no!' Saskia, looking panicky, crossed her hands rapidly in front of her. 'But he was going on about it last weekend. You could call his bluff and do it.'

'I'm not sure an orange veil would look right with that dress, love,' Marcia said.

'But if it was made of crystal organza and you wore it more like a stole—actually, that would look stunning.' Anna looked thoughtful. 'Especially if your hair's up and you wear finger-less elbow-length gloves and your bouquet's a simple sheaf of lilies. If you choose the material today, I can hem it for you.'

Isobel spread her hands. 'Well, as none of you will tell me anything, I'll just have to let you decide for me.'

Saskia grinned. 'And don't you just *hate* not being in charge?'

Isobel scowled. 'Alex called me a control freak, too.'

'You are,' Saskia said, laughing. 'You like everything just so.'

'It's called doing your research properly.' Isobel sighed. 'My colleagues all have invitations to the reception, but he's sworn them all to secrecy as well. Nobody will even give me a hint. It's driving me *insane*.'

'He's not going to tell you, so there's no point in stressing about it,' Saskia told her.

'So you've got everything now, apart from the gloves and the veil?' Marcia asked. 'Something old, something new, something borrowed and something blue?'

'I've got a new dress,' Isobel said. 'So that's one of them.'

'And you can borrow my gold bracelet—the one my parents gave me for my twenty-first,' Anna said. 'That takes care of old and borrowed. I'll bring it to you on your wedding morning.'

'And I'll deal with the blue,' Saskia said with a smile. 'Something tasteful, Bel, I promise.'

'Thank you. You've all gone to a lot of trouble over this.' There was a huge lump in Isobel's throat.

'That's because we love you,' Anna said, hugging her daughter. 'And we all want you to have the happiness you deserve. With Alex.'

Alex.

Her husband-to-be.

Who was equally convinced that everything would work out just fine.

She knew Alex was nothing like Gary. And, as Alex had pointed out, they were going into the marriage with their eyes wide open. Practical. Sensible. So why was the fear—the horrible feeling that everything was going to go pear-shaped—still dragging along behind her like a shadow?

Isobel managed to keep it away for the rest of the after-noon—just—while they went shopping for more shoes and the gloves to match her dress. Their last stop was to choose a length of shimmering flame-coloured crystal organza.

'Don't tell Alex about this,' she said. 'As he's keeping me in suspense about everything, I want this to be a surprise.'

'We won't let him see the dress, either,' Marcia promised.

'Thank you.'

'I'll take these,' Anna said, scooping up the bags contain-ing Isobel's dress, the shoes and the material for the wrap. 'I'll be helping you get ready, so I'll bring them with me—that way Alex won't see them before the big day.'

Isobel shivered. 'Mum, I…'

'Shh.' Anna kissed her gently. 'Of course you've got but-terflies in your stomach. It's only natural.'

They weren't butterflies. They were elephants, doing the cancan.

'But Alex is the right man for you,' Anna said softly. 'You love each other, so everything's going to be fine.'

Was it?

Isobel wasn't so sure—because they didn't love each other. Not in the way their family seemed to think they did.

But she forced herself to smile. 'Thanks, Mum.'

Over the weekend, Isobel found the perfect wedding present for Alex on the internet—a watch made of black ceramic, with no markers on the dial except for a diamond on the twelve. She discovered there was a stockist for the Swiss manufac-turer near the museum, so she dropped in on Monday lunch-time to buy it and have it wrapped. Then she transferred it to a plain bag so if Alex did spot it he wouldn't have a clue what she'd bought.

The next few days went by in a blur. And then it was the day before their wedding: her last day at work for over a week. Isobel ate a sandwich at her desk and used the time to try to get ahead of schedule with her work, but at the end of the day, when she'd planned to slip quietly away, Rita banged a spoon against a bottle of sparkling wine and the whole department focused on Isobel.

'You haven't got a wedding list,' Rita said, 'so we were flying a bit blind here, but I hope you like it.' She handed Isobel a beautifully wrapped box. 'Happy wedding, from all of us.'

Isobel carefully unwrapped it, and stared in delight when she opened the box to discover a fused-glass bowl, shading from light azure through to deep cobalt. 'It's gorgeous, Rita. Thank you. Thank you all so much.'

'Our pleasure,' Rita said, speaking on behalf of the department. 'See you tomorrow night.' She hugged Isobel. 'You've got a good man, there.' She lowered her voice. 'And he'll be so much better for you than He Who Should Not Be Named. You'll be happy with Alex. It shows in your face when you look at him—and when he looks at you.'

If only you knew, Isobel thought, but she smiled. 'Thanks, Rita.'

She went back to her flat, carefully protecting her parcel on the tube. Alex was waiting for her and kissed her hello. 'How was your day?'

'Lovely. Look what everyone in the department gave us as a wedding present.'

Alex inspected the bowl. 'That's gorgeous. I love the colours. And it'll look great in our new house.'

Isobel frowned. 'What new house?'

'The one we'll be looking at when we get back after the wedding. This flat only has one bedroom,' he reminded her, 'and if we're going to start a family we're going to need extra space.'

She lifted her chin. 'What if we can't have a family, Alex?'

'We'll face that if we have to.' He raised an eyebrow. 'My grandmother used to have a saying: "Never trouble trouble, until trouble troubles you." But if you want to think of it another way—with two of us, and the fact that I've got even more books than you have, we need more office space and more storage space. Which means a bigger place.'

'You are going to let me have a choice in this, aren't you? You're not going to steamroller me, the way you have about the wedding?'

'I'm not steamrollering you. I've been trying to *surprise*

you about the wedding,' Alex pointed out. 'I'm giving you a day to remember. Choosing a home's different—the place has to feel right for both of us, so we need to look at it together.'

'So you're telling me I have to put my flat on the market?'

He shook his head. 'Keep it as an investment. You can rent it out—the rent should cover your mortgage.'

She frowned. 'But yours is rented out, too. How on earth are we going to afford another flat between us?'

'Actually,' he said, 'my flat isn't going to be rented out any more. The letting agent rang me the other day and said the tenants wanted to know if I'd consider selling to them. Serendipity,' he said with a smile. 'Obviously I wanted to discuss it with you, first, before saying yes. But a bigger place would be sensible, wouldn't it?'

'I suppose so.' She bit her lip. 'Alex, my life feels as if it's been zooming along on a fairground ride—at a speed I can't control, spinning round just when I think I know where I'm going. A month ago, I was single and I thought you were in Turkey. Tomorrow, I'm marrying you—and in ten days' time you start an office job. And now you're telling me we're going to move house.'

'Right now it might seem we're going fast, but it's all going to be fine,' he told her softly, pulling her into his arms. 'And think of the fun we're going to have, choosing a new place together.'

'Hmm.' Isobel wasn't so sure. What he'd suggested was sensible, she knew—but she liked her flat. Liked it a *lot*. It had been her bolt-hole ever since she'd split up with Gary. And losing that security...

'Just trust me,' he said, holding her close. 'I'll call the trattoria and get them to deliver dinner while you pack—and then we'll go straight after dinner.'

'Go where?'

'To the place where we're getting married tomorrow.' He rolled his eyes. 'Pay attention, Mrs Richardson-to-be.'

'So we're not getting married in London?'

'No.' He smiled at her. 'Pasta, salad and garlic bread OK for dinner?'

It was much easier just to give in and go along with him when Alex was on a roll. And she adored Italian food anyway. 'Fine.'

'Good. Go and pack—I'd recommend just a few light clothes. If it turns cold where we are, then I'll buy you something warmer when we're there,' Alex said.

He was giving her absolutely no clue about where they were going—tonight or after the wedding. Though at least, she thought, he hadn't carried out his threat of packing for her.

She was still none the wiser about their destination when they left London, though when Alex turned onto the M4 she was fairly sure he was heading for the Cotswolds. It made sense that they'd get married near their respective families.

But then he took a different turning. 'Alex? Where are we—?'

'You'll know when we get there,' he said.

'You really are an infuriating man.'

He gave her a sunny smile. 'Indeedy.'

When he drove into Bath and parked outside a beautiful Georgian manor in the middle of the city, she blinked again. '*This* is where we're getting married?'

'Stop asking questions,' he said. 'We're staying here tonight.'

'Alex…' She swallowed. 'I know we're not exactly getting married for traditional reasons, but I'm not supposed to see you on the day of the wedding until the actual ceremony. It's bad luck.' She dragged in a breath. 'I saw Gary on the morning of the wedding.'

'Honey, that had nothing to do with why your marriage broke up. You just married a man who wasn't good enough for you and who let you down.' He stroked her face. 'I'm not Gary. This isn't a rerun of your first marriage, and I'm not going to let you down. But I had a feeling you'd be superstitious about this. Which is why we're having separate rooms— and I'm going to sneak out of your room and go to my own at precisely one minute to midnight.'

'So when do I see our mums and Saskia?' she asked.

'After your alarm call at six.'

'*Six?* Alex, that's the crack of dawn.'

'Just as well you're a morning person, then.' He paused. 'Bel, there's something I need to talk to you about.'

Ice trickled down her spine. 'What?'

'Don't look so worried.' He bent his head and stole a kiss. 'Just that you need to be on time tomorrow. I know it's traditional for the bride to be late, but if you're late tomorrow we'll have major problems.'

She frowned. 'So what time are we getting married?'

'Half past eight.'

'You're kidding! Why so early?'

'Tomorrow,' he said, 'all will be clear.'

'As mud,' she grumbled.

'Everyone else is staying at a different hotel.' He gave her a wicked little smile. 'So they don't cramp our style. But you'll see them in the morning. Our mums and Saskia are bringing your outfit with them.'

He signed them into the hotel, then carried their bags upstairs to her room.

There was a bottle of champagne on ice in her room.

Which had a king-size bed.

'Time for just you and me,' he said softly. 'And there's something I want to give you. A wedding gift.'

'Me, too.' She'd retrieved the watch from its hiding place and packed it in her suitcase before they'd left London.

He turned the lights down low, then opened the champagne and poured them both a glass before raising his own in a toast. 'To us.'

'To us,' she echoed.

He undid his suitcase, then gave her a gold box, beautifully tied with an orange ribbon. Isobel smiled, thinking about her organza wrap: her compromise on the flame-coloured Roman-style veil he'd been so keen on. Alex gave her a suspicious glance. 'What's that smile about?'

'Tomorrow,' she quoted back at him, 'all will be clear.'

'Oh, yes?' He laughed. 'Maybe I'll have to seduce it out of you.'

'You can try.'

'Is that a dare?' His eyes glittered.

She backtracked, fast. 'No.'

'OK. You can open it now, if you like.'

She did—and stared at the string of almost perfectly symmetrical black pearls. 'They're beautiful.' They had an incredible shimmering lustre—and although Isobel didn't know much about modern jewellery, she had a feeling they cost a small fortune. 'Alex. These are amazing. Thank you.'

'Happy wedding day,' he said softly. 'They're Tahitian, by the way.'

She tried them on. 'They feel gorgeous.'

'They look good on you,' he said with a smile. 'Maybe you can wear them tomorrow.'

'I will. They'll be perfect with my dress.' Gently, she took them off and put them back in the box, then retrieved the box from her own suitcase. 'And this is for you.'

He unwrapped it and blinked as he saw the black ceramic watch. 'Wow. This is fantastic.'

'I thought you'd like something high-tech and sophisticated,' she said.

He tried it on. 'It's perfect—thank you. And I'll wear it tomorrow.' He put it back in his box, then went to sit next to her on the bed. 'Come here. Let me thank you properly.'

'I need to thank you properly, too.'

He smiled, cupped her face in his hands and kissed her.

Their love-making was gentle, and so perfect that Isobel was near to tears.

At precisely two minutes to midnight, he climbed out of bed and pulled some clothes on.

And at precisely one minute to midnight, he kissed her goodnight. 'I'll see you tomorrow. Sleep well.' He stroked his face. 'And stop worrying. Everything's going to be just fine.'

CHAPTER NINE

ISOBEL slept really badly that night. Odd how she'd grown used to sleeping with someone again. The bed felt way too wide without Alex curled round her body, his arm wrapped round her waist and holding her close to him.

Every time she glanced at the clock, only a few minutes seemed to have gone past.

She'd just drifted into sleep when the phone shrilled.

Groggily, she reached out and felt for the phone, picked it up, and dropped it back on the cradle again.

The phone shrilled again.

This time she answered—more of a mumbled noise than an actual word, though she put the receiver to her ear.

'Rise and shine, honey. We're getting married in two and a half hours.'

'Alex? But…'

'It's not unlucky to talk to your bridegroom on the wedding morning, before you say it.' He laughed. 'Tomorrow, you can sleep in as late as you like.' His voice went husky. 'Because you might be a little bit busy tonight.'

'Oh, yes?'

'Later,' he promised. 'Later I'll carry you over the threshold. And there's going to be some serious ravishing in the bridal bed. But for now…go have your shower. Because I think you have visitors due in twenty-five minutes.'

She glanced at the clock. 'They'll be up already?'

'Their hotel is all of ten minutes' walk away, two minutes by taxi, and Saskia told me yesterday they're getting changed in your room—so I'd say the odds are they're already up or they've just hit the snooze button and they'll be up in five minutes. I'll see you at eight-thirty.'

'Eight-thirty,' she promised.

A shower and washing her hair made her feel a lot more awake. She'd just wrapped her hair in a towel and herself in the thick towelling robe provided by the hotel when there was a knock on her door. She opened it and Marcia, Anna and Saskia were all there, beaming at her and carrying an assortment of bags and cases.

'This is the plan. The mums sort the clothes and order breakfast by room service, I do your hair and make-up, and you're going to be the most beautiful bride ever,' Saskia informed her.

'Room service?' Isobel asked.

'Coffee and pastries. It's our family tradition to have cake for breakfast on red letter days,' Saskia said, smiling.

'In your dreams, you bad child.' Marcia laughed. 'I'm sorry, Anna. My daughter's a bad influence.'

'I hate to tell you this, but cake for breakfast sounds good to me as well,' Anna said, laughing back.

'*Pain au chocolat* and Danish pastries. Oh, and some orange juice so we can claim we've been healthy,' Saskia directed.

'Champagne and orange juice?' Anna suggested.

'Mmm, but we don't want her tipsy in case she falls into the—' Saskia clapped her hand over her mouth. 'I didn't say anything.'

'I could always tell Alex you told me anyway,' Isobel suggested.

Saskia cuffed her. 'Behave, or I'll accidentally on purpose stab you with a hair pin.'

Isobel didn't have a chance to start worrying about the wedding. What with a breakfast of pastries and Buck's Fizz, then the flowers arriving—a simple bouquet of cream Calla lilies that matched her cream silk shift dress perfectly—and her hair, nails and make-up being done, and everyone else getting changed, there wasn't a spare moment.

'Right. Time to get you dressed. Something old—and borrowed.' Anna handed her the bracelet.

'Thanks, Mum.'

'Something new—that's the dress. But before you do, the something blue.' Saskia fished in her bag and handed Isobel a box.

'A blue garter.'

'We won't make you flash your legs. Well, Alex might,' Saskia said with a grin.

'And we'll spare you the sixpence in your shoe—that'd be way too uncomfortable,' Marcia chipped in.

Saskia helped her into the dress and the gloves.

'And I need these.' Isobel took her pearls from the box.

'Oh, Bel—they're *gorgeous*,' Marcia sighed.

'Alex gave them to me as a wedding present,' she said shyly.

'They go perfectly with your dress,' Anna said. She brought out the organza stole and draped it round Isobel's shoulders. 'Oh, love. You look like a princess.'

Marcia took her camera from her handbag. 'Hold your flowers, Bel. That's it. Now smile.'

'You look…' Saskia blinked back tears. 'Oh, Bel. Today, you're really going to be my sister.'

'You used to tell your school friends that she was your twin, like Helen and Polly are twins,' Marcia said.

Anna's eyes were glittering with tears. 'The sister I never managed to give you, Bel.'

Isobel stared at her mother in surprise. It was something they'd never talked about, and as she'd grown up she'd simply assumed that because her parents were older, she'd been a 'happy accident' late in life rather than a planned baby.

So did this mean her mother had wanted more children? Or even that she'd had trouble conceiving—had had miscarriages, the same way that Isobel herself had? 'Mum…'

Anna shook her head. 'This isn't the time and the place to talk about it. But just as long as you know how much your father and I love you. How proud we are of you. And how happy we are that you and Alex are together.'

Isobel swallowed hard. 'I think I'm going to cry.'

'Don't you dare. You'll smudge your make-up. And Alex will scalp us if we deliver his bride in anything less than smile mode,' Saskia said quickly.

The phone rang; Marcia answered, then nodded. 'Thank you.' As the others turned to her in enquiry she said, 'That was the wedding car.'

'Wedding car? So where exactly are we going?' Isobel asked.

'It's more than our lives are worth to tell you,' Marcia said. 'But everyone else is meeting us there.'

Alex had hired an old-fashioned Rolls-Royce. And when the car pulled up outside Bath Abbey, Isobel shook her head. 'No. This can't be right. No way can he have booked the Abbey. They wouldn't marry us, not when I'm divorced.'

'It's not the Abbey,' Anna said gently, squeezing her hand. 'You'll love this.'

'Then where…?'

Enlightenment dawned when they reached the entrance to the old Roman baths. 'I don't believe he managed to organise this.'

'They're open to the public during the day, so the only time you can get married here is half past eight in the morning,' Saskia explained. 'Which is how come you had to be up at the crack of dawn.'

'I... Oh, Lord.' Isobel was lost for words.

'Smile,' Saskia directed, 'or my brother will scalp me.'

'We could've walked here, but Alex wanted to string it out to the last possible second,' Marcia said. She laughed. 'You know my son. He always takes things further than anyone else.'

'You can say that again,' Isobel said fervently.

The torches around the great pool were lit and the steam was rising. The water was pure aqua—the same colour as the bowl her colleagues had bought them. And that, Isobel thought, was probably no coincidence.

And then she saw Alex.

She'd known he was teasing her when he'd threatened to wear his battered Akubra or a toga. But she really hadn't expected this. He was wearing a morning suit: a black tailcoat and pinstriped trousers with a white wing-collar shirt and a gold waistcoat. And his cravat matched her stole exactly. The rest of the wedding party were dressed in similar style, and they all had a lily as their buttonhole.

For a moment, she could believe that she and Alex really were getting married for love. He looked absolutely stunning and, when he walked towards her, smiling, her heart felt as if it had done a weird kind of flip.

'That dress is perfect. Simple and classic and letting your beauty shine through. The gloves are pretty sexy, too. You look amazing,' he said softly.

'You look pretty stunning yourself.'

He smiled. 'Note—no toga, and no hat.'

She indicated her stole. 'And I've got the flame-coloured veil you asked for. Sort of.'

He laughed. 'I like it. And I like your hair up like that.' He leaned forward and whispered, 'And I'm really looking forward to taking it down later tonight.'

A shiver of pure desire rippled through her. 'Later.' She glanced round at the registrar and their family, sitting there with such love and such joy on their faces.

And Alex had been the one to make this all happen.

'Thank you, Alex, for doing this. It's just…' She could feel tears welling up.

He looked alarmed. 'Don't cry, Bel.'

'They're happy tears,' she hastened to reassure him.

'Even so.' He took her hand, raised it to his mouth and kissed it. 'Let's go and get married.'

'I can't believe we're getting married on a two-thousand-year-old warm pavement.'

He smiled. 'I told you it was going to be different.'

'It's perfect, Alex.'

She walked with him over to the table where the registrar was sitting; Alex held her hand very, very tightly as the registrar welcomed them all.

'I declare I know of no legal reason why I, Alexander Tobias Richardson, may not be joined in marriage to Isobel Anna Martin,' Alex said at the registrar's prompting.

She repeated his declaration.

Then he turned to her. Held both hands. Looked her straight in the eye. 'I, Alexander, take you, Isobel, to be my lawful wedded wife.'

She swallowed hard. 'I, Isobel, take you, Alexander, to be my lawful wedded husband.'

Then Saskia came to the front, carrying Flora, who was holding a basket containing the wedding rings.

Alex took the smaller one and slid it onto her finger. 'With my heart, I pledge to you all that I am. With this ring I marry you and join my life to yours.'

And even though he didn't mention love in his vows, she knew he meant what he said.

Just as she meant it when she took the other ring and slid it onto his ring finger. 'With my heart, I pledge to you all that I am. With this ring I marry you and join my life to yours.'

She barely heard the registrar's speech; the only thing that she could focus on was Alex's wide smile when the registrar said, 'You may kiss the bride.'

He did.

When they'd signed the register, it was time for photographs. Then they went back to the hotel, where there were more photographs in the garden and Alex's nephews took great delight in throwing rose petals over them—and then brunch, which Alex had arranged in a private dining room.

'So where are the speeches?' Polly asked.

'We're not doing any. We're together, we're married, we're happy. End of story.' Alex gestured to his nephews, who were busily playing with the train set he'd had put in the room earlier. 'And the kids won't want to sit through long speeches.'

'They won't mind. They're quite happy playing, thanks to their genius uncle,' Helen said.

Alex laughed. 'I can remember sitting through weddings at their age and being bored out of my mind. I thought they'd like something a bit more interesting to do.'

'They love it,' Poppy confirmed.

'Come on. Don't cheat us,' Helen wheedled. 'Speech.'

'No need.' Alex gave her his most charming smile. 'As I said. We're together, we're married, we're happy. Everyone knows how we met—and everyone knows everything about both of us. So there's nothing more to say.'

'Actually, as the father of the bride, I'd like to say something,' Stuart said diffidently. 'I found this lovely blessing on the internet. I'm sorry it's not Roman—it's Apache—but I thought the words were lovely.'

'Go on, Dad,' Isobel said.

Stuart stood up, took a piece of paper from the inside pocket of his jacket, and unfolded it. With a tender look at Isobel, he said:

'May the sun bring you new happiness by day;
May the moon softly restore you by night;
May the rain wash away your worries
And the breeze blow new strength into your being,
And all the days of your life
May you walk gently through the world and know its
beauty.
Now you will feel no rain,
For each of you will be the shelter for each other.
Now you will feel no cold,
For each of you will be the warmth for the other.
Now you are two persons,
But there is only one life before.
Go now to your dwelling place to enter
Into the days of your life together.
And may your days be good and long upon the earth.'

Everyone clapped loudly.

'Hear, hear,' Marcia said. 'Stuart, that's so lovely.'

Isobel had a lump in her throat. She glanced at Alex, who tightened his fingers round hers.

'Thank you, Stuart,' Alex said.

Even his eyes were smiling, Isobel thought. As if he'd married her for real.

Well, it was legally real. Just not the great love match everyone believed it was.

Tom stood up, next. 'I'm more of a figures man than a words man,' he said ruefully, 'so I can't come up with anything anywhere near as pretty as Stuart. So I'm going just to keep it short and sweet. Welcome to the family, Bel—though we've thought of you as part of our family for years anyway, we're so pleased that you're officially ours now. And may you both be very happy. I'd like everyone to join me in raising their glasses in a toast. Bel and Alex.'

'Bel and Alex,' everyone echoed, raising their glasses of champagne.

In response, Alex kissed Isobel. Very, very thoroughly.

CHAPTER TEN

'SEEING as our dads have made such nice speeches,' Alex said, 'maybe I will say a few words.'

'About time, too,' Helen teased.

'I just want to thank you all for being here. For sharing our special day—and for all the help beforehand, especially from our mums and Saskia. I know it's traditional for the bride and groom to give gifts to their parents and ring-bearer and what have you—but I loathe giving gifts in public,' Alex said, 'so you'll find our thanks to you back in your respective hotel rooms. And the train set is for the boys to keep, by the way,' he added to his middle sisters. 'There should be enough track and trains for it to be a decent set each when split in two.'

'Alex, that's so sweet of you.' Polly smiled at him. 'Thank you.'

'And as everyone was up at the crack of dawn,' Alex continued, 'I suggest an afternoon nap before the reception this evening. You're welcome to stay here for more champagne or coffee, but I want some quiet time alone with my bride before tonight.'

'Quiet time alone,' Saskia said, rolling her eyes. 'Yeah. We all know what *that* means.'

Alex laughed. 'I said quiet time, not wedding night.' He

raised his glass. 'To you all. Because Bel and I are lucky to have the best family in the world.'

'Oh, you charmer,' Saskia said, but she was looking misty-eyed. And Isobel had too big a lump in her throat to speak.

Alex had a quick word with the butler, then whisked Isobel off to the garden and found a quiet table and chairs beneath a tree. 'We're going to do a very English thing, now, and have tea in the garden.'

'That's fine by me.' She smiled at him. 'You've made it the perfect day.' And very different from her first marriage. He'd made it so much easier for her, because there were no points of comparison. 'And this ring is beautiful.' A layer of white gold sandwiched between yellow gold.

'I'm glad you like it.'

Something in his eyes made her wonder. 'What aren't you telling me?'

He gave her an enigmatic smile. 'Doesn't matter. Bel, you look amazing in that dress. Especially with the, ahem, orange veil.'

'It's a stole, and you know it,' she corrected with a grin. 'You look pretty amazing yourself. I thought you hated wearing suits.'

'I do.' He shrugged. 'But you nixed the toga and my normal clothes just aren't appropriate today.' He reached over to run his thumb along her lower lip. 'I did think about taking you for a spa this afternoon—but I didn't want to mess up your hair or your make-up before this evening.'

'I don't know if I dare ask what you've planned for this evening.'

He laughed. 'It's a surprise. But one I think you'll like.'

'Continuing the Roman theme?'

'Might be.' He raised an eyebrow. 'Just think yourself lucky they throw confetti rather than walnuts at the bride and groom nowadays.'

'You've gone to so much trouble, Alex.'

'You're worth it,' he said simply.

For a moment, Isobel thought he was going to tell her he loved her.

But she knew that Alex didn't believe in love.

And she didn't, either. She wasn't going to let her heart be broken again. He was absolutely right to be practical about this. Deep friendship and spectacular sex were a good basis for a marriage. Something that wouldn't crumble—unlike love. And if they couldn't have a family...he'd still be there for her. He wouldn't walk away.

'This,' Alex said after the waitress had brought their tea, 'is the life.'

Isobel scoffed. 'You'd far rather be pottering around ruins with a camera and someone who'd talk to you about the history of the place.'

'Well, yes,' he admitted. 'But that's hardly an option today.'

'What time do we have to be at the reception?'

He raised an eyebrow. 'Are you worrying again?'

'No—just wondering how much free time we have.'

He glanced at his watch. 'Ages. We don't have to be there until seven. Which means leaving here about ten to, if you don't mind walking.'

She smiled. 'Walking's fine with me.'

'Obviously we'll be expected to dance together, but we can get away with just the traditional first dance if you really hate it.'

The first dance. That feeling of floating on air—and, despite being in a crowded place, there being nobody there except her husband. 'Just as long as you haven't picked the same song as I had with Gary.'

'Hardly. Apart from the fact we're having a string quartet...'

'A string quartet?'

He laughed. 'They're going to switch halfway through to pop stuff. Don't worry. It'll be fine.'

'I don't think I've ever seen you dance. You didn't dance at Saskia's wedding—or Helen's, or Polly's.' Or her own wedding to Gary, now she thought about it.

He shrugged. 'It's not something I do very much.'

'So you can't dance?'

'I didn't say I can't. Just that I don't.' He raised an eyebrow. 'Worried that I'll have two left feet and ruin your shoes?'

'No.' *Yes.*

Alex stood up, took her hand and pulled her to her feet. 'OK. Practice run.' He held her close, then began to sing a ballad very softly as he danced with her, swaying perfectly in time to the beat.

'I had no idea you had such a nice voice, Alex.' He'd never sung along to the radio whenever they'd travelled in a car together.

'Thank you, Bel.' He pulled back and gave her a mock bow. 'So I take it you're no longer worried that I'm going to bruise your toes.'

She smiled. 'You have a good sense of rhythm—but that wasn't really dancing.'

He laughed. 'If you're expecting Fred Astaire or Patrick Swayze, forget it. That's as much as I do. And only on very, very special occasions.'

So was he saying that today was very special for him?

She didn't dare ask.

When they returned to their table, Alex kept the conversation very firmly on the topic of history. Which suited Isobel just fine: it kept her mind well off dangerous emotions.

But she could see he was looking fidgety. Eventually, she reached over and took his hand. 'Alex. You want to go exploring, don't you?'

'I'm perfectly happy sitting here with you, relaxing.'

'Liar.' She smiled at him. 'We're only a short walk away from the baths. I haven't been there for ages.'

He coughed. 'All of five hours, by my reckoning.'

'I mean as a tourist.'

'Isn't this a bit of a busman's holiday? A busman's honeymoon, even?' he teased. 'Bel, I can't go wandering round Bath dressed like *this*.' He fluttered his fingers at his morning suit.

'How about we go and change? Nobody's going to know.'

'You can get away with staying as you are—leave the stole and gloves here and you look like a wedding guest killing a bit of time before the ceremony.'

'That goes for you, too.'

He ran a finger round the collar of his shirt. 'How about I ditch the jacket, cravat and waistcoat?'

She couldn't be hard-hearted enough to make him stay in an outfit he obviously loathed. 'Deal. Your room or mine?'

'Just hand your stole to me and I'll sort it.'

She frowned. 'What's the big deal about not letting me see the room?'

'Because,' he said softly, 'I want the first time you see it to be when I carry you over the threshold. To our bed.'

The thought sent a shiver of desire through her.

'Hold that thought,' he said, and took the organza stole and her gloves.

He returned a few minutes later, wearing just the white shirt and dark trousers. 'Sure you're OK to walk in those shoes?'

'Would I buy shoes I couldn't walk in?' she asked.

He laughed. 'Course not. Practical to the last, my Bel.' His eyes glittered, and he sang the first verse of 'Michelle', changing the name to 'Isobel'.

She groaned. 'That's *terrible*, Alex. Come on. Let's go exploring.'

They spent the rest of the afternoon wandering round Bath, starting with a tour of the Roman baths.

'Just think. We got married here, a few hours ago,' Alex whispered, sliding his arm round her and holding her close when they got to the Great Bath.

Married. She still hadn't quite taken it in. And despite the ring sitting on her finger, she didn't *feel* married. This felt like playing hookey with her friend and lover to do something they both enjoyed.

Alex insisted on playing tourist afterwards and having afternoon tea in the Pump Room. 'Tea, yes. A glass of warm spa water from the fountain—no,' Isobel said.

'Chicken,' he teased.

'Be my guest if you want to try the water,' she teased back, 'but I've done it before and, I warn you, it's vile.'

After tea, they wandered hand in hand round the Circus, admiring the Georgian houses. 'I'd love a house like that,' Isobel said wistfully. 'All high ceilings and masses of light.'

'We can if you want,' Alex said.

She wrinkled her nose. 'Think of the commute to work every day.'

'You're right—it'd be too much.' He looked thoughtful. 'You know, we could buy a flat in a Georgian town house somewhere like Bloomsbury. High ceilings and lots of light, like these ones.'

'And a price tag to suit.'

He squeezed her hand. 'Actually, we can afford it, otherwise I wouldn't have suggested it.'

'You might be able to, but I can't. And I'm paying half the mortgage,' she added swiftly.

'Bel, don't be difficult. Now you're officially married to

me, what's mine is yours. Actually, it makes sense for us to live in Bloomsbury—it means we both have a reasonable commute. And if you like the area…'

'I do,' she admitted.

'Then let's do it.'

She looked up at the mellow stone houses. 'Are you sure?'

'Yes. We're not in a chain, so once we've found a place we both like we can persuade the vendors to let us have early possession. They win because they've sold—and we win because we have the house we want. Result.'

'Persuasion's your middle name, isn't it?' she asked wryly.

He laughed. 'So that's a yes, then?'

She nodded. 'That's a yes. And thank you.'

He spun her round to face him and kissed her thoroughly. 'We'll get ourselves on some mailing lists in the morning before we go to the airport.'

Finally, they went back to their hotel. Alex glanced at his watch. 'As we ought to be there first to welcome everyone, we'd better leave in a minute. Do you need to freshen up?'

'Just my make-up. I'd guess that I don't have any lipstick left on.'

'You kissed me as much as I kissed you,' he pointed out.

She laughed. 'So are we in my room now or yours?'

He evaded the question. 'Can't you just do what girls normally do and whip a mirror and lipstick out of your bag?'

She spread her hands. 'Funnily enough, I don't have a bag on me. Which means my lipstick is upstairs.'

'I'll fetch it.'

'Alex, it'd be quicker if I—'

'No,' he cut in. 'Not until I carry you over the threshold.'

He returned a couple of minutes later, holding her make-up bag and compact mirror. When Isobel had refreshed her make-up, he took the bag back to their room, then came back downstairs wearing the jacket, waistcoat and cravat again.

'Ready?' he asked.

'Ready,' she confirmed.

And this time she wasn't that surprised when he led her back to the Roman Baths.

'I should've guessed,' she said.

He shrugged. 'I had to carry the theme through, didn't I?'

'So this string quartet…is it going to play Roman music?'

He laughed. 'Considering nobody knows exactly what Roman music was like…no. They're going to play ordinary chamber music. Bach, Vivaldi, some Mozart.'

The musicians were playing a violin concerto when Alex and Isobel walked in. That teamed with the backdrop of the Roman baths in the evening, lit by torches and with steam rising from the water, Isobel found incredibly moving. There was a table full of glasses and champagne bottles in ice buckets, another table laden with food, and smaller tables and chairs dotted around where people could sit and chat.

'It's perfect,' Isobel whispered.

Their family were the first guests to arrive. Stuart shook Alex's hand warmly and hugged Isobel. 'That paperweight was beautiful, darling. Thank you.'

'Our pleasure,' Isobel said, hugging him back. 'Help yourself to champagne, Dad.'

Their mothers and Saskia were equally delighted with their bouquets, and Tom seemed pleased with his paperweight. 'Every time I see it on my desk I'll think of today. Thank you both.'

'Polly and I didn't do anything to help,' Helen said, 'so we didn't really deserve a present.'

'We didn't want to leave anyone out. Besides, I thought if we bought you enough posh chocolate, you might not nag me for five seconds or so,' Alex replied with a grin.

'Oh, you!' She cuffed him playfully. 'Bel, I hope you're going to reform him.'

'She likes me just as I am—don't you, Bel?' Alex retorted.

Isobel rolled her eyes. 'I don't think anyone could change your brother anyway, Helen.'

More and more people arrived to be welcomed, shake hands and wish them well. Some of Alex's former colleagues had flown in from Turkey; others had travelled the length of the country to be there. Most of Isobel's department came from London, as well as old friends of the family from nearby.

The guest list—at least on her side—wasn't much different from her first wedding, Isobel thought. Except this time she wasn't wearing rose-coloured glasses. And this time...this time, she really hoped everything would last.

CHAPTER ELEVEN

ALEX caught the attention of the first violinist, and gave the signal for the first dance. The arrangement he'd asked them to do especially for tonight. A song that definitely hadn't been played at Isobel's first wedding: and one he knew she liked.

'Ladies and gentlemen, I give you the bride and groom,' the first violinist said, and began playing.

He could see in the way that Isobel's eyes widened that she recognised the tune instantly. And even though this was an instrumental arrangement of 'Time in a Bottle', he was well aware that she knew all the lyrics to the song. She'd know how appropriate it was.

'Alex. This is—' Isobel began.

'Shh,' he said, taking her in his arms. Thanks to her high heels, if he leaned forward just a little he could dance cheek to cheek with her.

If he believed in love, he'd say that right now that was the way he felt about Bel. His friend. His lover. His bride.

The thought made him freeze. Last time he'd believed in love, it had gone so badly wrong. That was why he'd never let his heart get involved again—why his relationships had always been for fun, and he'd walked away before they had a chance to get serious.

With Isobel, it was different.

He'd always liked her. Even when they'd been children, she'd been quieter than his sisters, more serious, and he hadn't minded her tagging along behind him. In his teens and twenties, he'd found her easy to talk to, good company—particularly as she shared his love of history. She'd been the one who'd encouraged him to submit his articles to a Sunday broadsheet. And she'd been the first person he'd called to tell about the offer of the television series.

The more he thought about it, the more he realised how important Isobel had been in his life.

And that made it even more essential that he didn't fall in love with her. Because he didn't want this to go wrong. He wanted to come home to her at the end of the day, moan about the paperwork and let her tease him out of his bad mood. He wanted to share his discoveries with her, knowing that she'd be as excited about them as he was.

And he wanted a little girl with Isobel's huge brown eyes and shy smile—a girl he could carry round on his shoulders and who'd adore him as much as he adored her. A girl he could teach to find fossils at the beach and dig trenches in their garden.

It shook Alex that he was actually starting to feel broody—that he wanted a baby as much as he knew Isobel did. So when the song ended, he kissed her lightly on the cheek. He needed space between them. Right now. And there was only one way to do it nicely. 'That's my dancing done for tonight. Better circulate, I suppose, before people start grumbling that I'm monopolising the bride.'

Though even as he worked the room, chatted with friends, he was very aware of exactly where Isobel was—almost as if some invisible cord bound him to her. Every so often, he looked across at her and she'd suddenly glance up, catch his eye and smile at him. And every time that happened, it made him feel odd—as if his heart had skipped a beat.

Eventually, he couldn't stay away from her any more. She was talking to her colleagues when he came to stand behind her, slid his arms round her waist and pulled her back against him. Just as everyone would expect him to. And although Isobel would think that he was playing a part, he knew he wasn't. He needed to hold her. To feel grounded.

'This was an inspired setting for the day, Alex,' Rita told him.

'Considering my wife spends half her working life dressed as a Roman matron, we could hardly have had the wedding anywhere else,' Alex said with a smile. 'Will you excuse me, Rita? I need a quick word with the bride.' He ushered Isobel over to a quiet corner. 'Bel, we've got an early start tomorrow. It might be a good idea to say our goodbyes and sneak out now.'

'An early start? As early as today's?' she queried.

'Not *quite*.' He stroked her bare nape. 'But I've had enough of being sociable.'

She nodded. 'And it's a bit of a strain, living up to everyone's expectations and pretending to be in love.'

It was even more of a strain trying not to fall in love with her, if she only knew it. 'We don't need love. We're better off without it.' And he knew he was trying to convince himself as much as he was trying to convince her. 'We have a solid friendship—' he nuzzled her ear '—and great sex. It's an unbeatable combo.'

'Definitely.'

Was it his imagination, or did she sound a bit wistful?

But weddings did that to women.

Especially brides.

So of course Bel wasn't falling in love with him.

And he'd be very, very stupid if he hoped that she was. Falling in love would be the first step to their marriage falling apart.

They quietly said their goodbyes, then sneaked out of the reception and walked hand in hand back to their hotel.

'So. Just you and me,' Alex said when the lift doors closed behind them. 'There's something I've been wanting to do all day.' And maybe making love with her would clear his head. Bring him back to normal.

Her eyes widened. 'Alex, we're in a lift. It's *public*.'

'I can't see anyone else here.' He spun her round so she was facing the mirror at the back of the lift. 'But I'll defer to your wishes and keep your clothes on. For now.' He ran his finger lightly along the zip at the back of her dress. 'But I'm looking forward to sliding this down. And kissing every inch of skin I reveal—all the way down your spine,' he whispered. 'And then…' He splayed his palms on her abdomen. 'Then I'm going to touch you, Bel.' He slid his hands upwards until he was cupping her breasts. 'I'm going to touch you here.' He rubbed his thumbs over her nipples, feeling them start to harden through her clothes. 'And here.' He slid one hand down until the heel of his hand was just above the opening of her thighs, pressing against her. 'I'm going to touch you. Taste you. Tease you until you're absolutely desperate for me.'

Her mouth had parted, her colour had risen and her eyes were glittering with desire.

Good.

Just how he wanted her.

'Hold that thought,' he whispered as the lift doors opened behind them.

He laced his fingers through hers and led her down the corridor to their room for the night. Pushed the cardkey through the lock. Bent slightly so he could scoop one arm under her knees and lift her up in his arms. 'Tradition,' he said as he carried her over the threshold.

Her eyes went wide as she saw the four-poster. 'I wasn't expecting this.'

'I thought I'd better be traditional about something.' He paused. 'And now it's time for something else traditional. The wedding night. I'm going to make love with my bride. Very, *very* slowly.'

He gently tweaked the stole from her shoulders and dropped it on the bed. Then he spun her round and drew the zip downwards. Slowly. Prolonging the teasing for both of them. He dipped his head to kiss the nape of her neck, then trailed kisses down her spine as he drew the zip downwards. He eased the dress over her shoulders, hooking her bra straps out of the way at the same time so he could bare her shoulders completely, and kissed his way along to the curve of her neck. He let the dress slide to the floor, and she stepped out of it; he picked it up and hung it over the back of a chair, then looked at her. She was wearing only her bra with the straps pulled down, a pair of lace-topped hold-up stockings, a blue lacy garter, and the flimsiest pair of silk knickers. She still had her back to him—and he'd never seen anything so enticing in his entire life. 'Now there's a view,' he said. He'd aimed for teasing, but his voice sounded slightly husky to his own ears. Too breathy. Too desperate. Not good.

He took out the pins from her hair. 'I want this down.' He ran his fingers through it. Her hair was soft and silky, and curled slightly round his fingers. 'And you smell lovely.' He leaned closer. 'Orange blossom again.'

She turned round. 'And you're wearing too much.' Her voice, too, sounded slightly husky. Breathy.

He was pretty sure she needed this as much as he did. 'So you're saying you want me naked?'

She gave the tiniest, tiniest shiver. 'Yes.'

'OK, then.' He took off his jacket and hung it over the back of the chair with her dress. The waistcoat was next; he undid each button before shrugging it off and dropping it on top of his jacket. The cravat…well, hopefully she wouldn't notice that his hands were shaking. And then he stopped. Raised an eyebrow. 'My fingers ache.'

She smiled, clearly picking up on the game. 'So you're saying you want a hand?'

He smiled. 'I'm saying I want you to undress me. Preferably five seconds ago.'

She sashayed over to him, and his heart skipped a beat. When she undid the buttons of his shirt, he couldn't keep his hands off her any longer; he curved his hands over her buttocks, drawing her closer.

Her eyes widened slightly when she felt his erection pressing against her. And then she gave him a sensual smile, and slid one hand across his pectorals. 'Mmm, you feel nice.'

He made short work of undoing his shirt cuffs and dropped the shirt on the floor.

She laughed. 'You've stopped being neat, then.'

'Yep.' He had no intention of doing anything that took him a millimetre away from her or a millisecond longer before he could wrap her body round his.

She undid his trousers, sliding the zipper down as slowly as he'd done with the zip of her dress. Then she drew one fingertip along his length.

'Oh, if teasing's on the menu…' He stepped out of his trousers and removed his socks, then unsnapped her bra with one hand. He had no idea where the lacy garment fell and he really didn't care—what he needed right now was to touch her.

Taste her. He dipped his head and took one nipple into his mouth.

She gasped his name and threaded her fingers through his hair, urging him on.

He didn't need any more hints. He simply picked her up, carried her over to the four-poster bed, and laid her back against the pillows before kneeling between her thighs. He placed the flat of his palms against her waist; Lord, her skin was soft. And he wanted to touch her even more intimately. He moulded his hands over the curve of her hips, her thighs, as if learning her shape for the first time. Then he hooked a finger under her blue garter. 'I'm glad you're wearing stockings.' It was incredibly sexy.

He traced the lacy edges of the hold-up tops with his fingertip. 'I love the contrast between this and your skin. Rough against smooth.' He took her hand and pressed it against his jaw. 'Rough against smooth,' he whispered again and dipped his head to draw a line of kisses along her collar-bone, just below where the black pearls circled her neck, then down between her breasts. He circled her navel with the tip of his tongue, and he could feel her quivering in anticipation; clearly she needed this as much as he did. He slid one hand between her thighs, cupping her sex through her knickers. 'These are too much of a barrier, wouldn't you agree?'

Her beautiful brown eyes grew darker. 'Yes.'

'Allow me a barbarian moment.' Still keeping eye contact, he ripped the sides of her knickers and disposed of them in two seconds flat.

'Oh, my God. Alex, I don't believe you just did that!' She stared at him, looking shocked. 'You actually ripped my knickers off! And they were silk, I'll have you know.'

He shrugged. 'So I'll buy you some more. Not that you'll actually be needing to wear any for the next week...' He stroked her stocking tops again. 'These can stay. And the pearls.'

She shook her head. 'I don't want them spoiled.'

'They won't be.'

She looked pained. 'Alex…'

He smiled. 'You're so practical.'

'That's why you married me. Because I'm settled and boring.'

'Settled, yes. Boring…never.' He kissed her lightly on the mouth, removed the pearls and put them in their box. 'OK now?'

She coughed. 'You've forgotten something.'

'What?'

'Those.' She nodded at his close-fitting jersey boxers. 'Unless you want me to rip them off.'

As he'd just done to her. He laughed. 'Wrong material. It'd take you way too long.' He removed his boxers and came to lie next to her. 'I'm entirely in your hands, *uxor mea*.'

'Are you, now?' She ran the tip of one finger down his sternum, following the line of arrowing hair down his abdomen, then deliberately traced the outline of his erection against his skin, keeping five millimetres away from actually touching his shaft.

She was driving him crazy.

'No teasing,' he warned.

'You said you were in my hands,' she reminded him.

'Your hands aren't anywhere near close enough to where I want them.'

'And where might that be, *maritus meus*?'

'That's more than enough teasing, Isobel Richardson.' He pulled her on top of him so she was straddling him, then shifted so that the tip of his penis was against her entrance. Then he laced his fingers through hers. 'Here will do quite nicely.'

She sucked in a breath. 'Alex.'

'Isobel.' He tilted his pelvis, and gently eased inside. 'Better. *Much* better.' Just where he needed to be. Losing himself inside her, the warmth surrounding him.

She rocked against him and began to move, so slowly that he ached. And just when he could bear it no longer, her control seemed to snap and she gripped his hands, moving over him rapidly.

A shiver of pure bliss spread through him. 'Bel. You feel fantastic. Like silk wrapped round me. And I...'

He just about managed to stop himself saying the words—words that scared the hell out of him, and might scare her well away from him. Instead, he sat up, still inside her, and held her close. Kissed her so that his treacherous mouth wouldn't have the chance to betray him. He felt the very moment that her body went still, poised on the edge of climax—and then his was rippling through him, too. He held her tightly, as if he were drowning and she were the only thing keeping him afloat; her arms were wrapped just as tightly around him.

'And now,' he said softly, when he was able to speak again, 'we're really married.'

CHAPTER TWELVE

ISOBEL woke briefly in the night. For a moment she was disoriented, wondering where she was; then she became aware of Alex's deep, regular breathing. His body was spooned round hers and his arm was wrapped round her waist, holding her close to him. Protected, safe.

When room service woke them in the morning, Alex switched from being her serious, intense lover of the night before to his usual teasing, charming self. He poured her coffee, then buttered some croissants and shared them with her, feeding her alternate bites and deliberately smudging jam against her mouth and leaning forward so he could lick it off.

He carried her to the shower after breakfast and Isobel thought he was going to join her; but then he set her down on her feet and stole a kiss. 'I'd better leave you to it. Because if I do what I really want to do right now, we're going to be late—and that's a bad idea.'

'So where are we going?'

'On honeymoon.'

He refused to give her any more detailed answer than that, and fobbed off every single question until they were actually at the airport.

The moment their flight was called and he stood up, pulling her to her feet, she knew where they were going.

'Naples? We're going to Pompeii?'

'And Herculaneum.' He smiled. 'I told you that you'd love it.'

Just as much as she knew he would. Wandering around ancient ruins was Alex's idea of the perfect holiday—just as it was hers.

When they finally arrived in Naples, she discovered that he'd found them an apartment in an ancient *palazzo* in the old quarter. Again, he insisted on carrying her over the threshold.

The apartment was gorgeous. High ceilings and lots of light, everything painted light colours, with terracotta flooring and voile curtains and white and gold and terracotta roses on the table. She looked out of the window to discover a balcony with a view of the bay and Vesuvius.

'This is wonderful, Alex. Absolutely perfect.'

'Good. Because there's something we need to do before we unpack.' He picked her up again and carried her over the threshold of their bedroom.

'Alex!'

'They eat late, in Naples. And when in Rome—well, Naples…' he quipped. 'So it doesn't matter if we go out late.'

It was very late by the time they went out for dinner. But there was something magical, Isobel thought, about sitting on a terrace overlooking the sea and watching the lights glittering against the night.

And it was the perfect week. They breakfasted on milky coffee and pastries in small cafés, and spent the mornings wandering round museums and churches before having a light lunch at one of the pavement cafés. Then Alex insisted that they needed a siesta, where they'd make love in their room with the afternoon light filtering through the voile curtains.

As Alex had promised, they spent a day at Herculaneum and another in Pompeii—and Isobel wouldn't have wanted to share this with anyone else but Alex. They wandered hand in hand through the village, looking at the frescos and the fountain covered in glass and shell mosaics and the statue of the dancing faun in a courtyard, and talking, talking, talking.

'It's nice to see a couple still like honeymooners after being together so many years,' an elderly tourist said to them with a smile.

Alex and Isobel looked at each other.

'Actually,' Alex said gently, 'we are honeymooners. We only got married at the weekend.'

'Oh!' The old lady flushed. 'I do apologise. It's just that I've been overhearing you talking, and you finish each other's sentences. It reminds me of how it was with my late husband and me—and we were together for forty years.'

'You're right in one sense. We've known each other for a lot of years,' Isobel said, reaching out to touch her hand.

'It just took you a while to realise how you felt about each other, hmm?'

It had taken Isobel a while to realise how she felt about Alex—not that she would tell him, because he'd run a mile. And as for how Alex felt about her... He cared. He just didn't believe in love. Though Isobel didn't have the heart to correct the old lady. 'Yes.'

'Congratulations, my dears. And may you have a very happy life together.'

It was all too easy to fall under the spell of romance in Naples—especially the day Alex took her out to the Blue Grotto at Capri, a fairytale cave bathed in iridescent turquoise light. Although his plans for the next day, a hike up Vesuvius to see the crater, brought her back to earth. 'I didn't realise I was that unfit,' she said when they finally reached the top and took a break from the climb.

'It's a fair bit steeper than anything you're used to in London—unless you take the stairs instead of the escalator on the tube,' he said, 'which you're too idle to do.'

'Idle? Pah. Just because you're used to hauling yourself in and out of trenches, showing off your biceps like some gym gorilla.'

'Any time you want to join me, honey, I could always use a research assistant.' He blew her a kiss.

Their last couple of days in Naples were idyllic. Good food, incredible surroundings and spectacular sex.

And then it was back to London. Back to real life.

Alex started his new job and seemed to love it. But she noticed his hours gradually stretched until he was working late every single night.

But that was Alex. He'd always been a workaholic.

And the fact that he hadn't mentioned babies since they were back from Italy...

She pushed the hurt aside. He'd said they should take it as it came; he'd even talked about his grandmother's saying about not troubling trouble. Maybe she should take her lead from him and forget about it.

But the longing wouldn't go away. Every day, it got stronger.

He took two days off when they moved from her flat to the place they'd found in Bloomsbury—one with high ceilings, lots of light, and vendors who were more than happy to move out early. Though Isobel was the one to go back to the Cotswolds a couple of days later to sort out his stuff in the attic at his parents' house.

'Typical Alex,' was Marcia's response, rolling her eyes. 'I don't think you'll ever change him.'

'He's really busy at work,' Isobel said. 'I'm sorry.'

'It's not your fault, love.' Marcia patted her hand. 'And you get him to ring me a lot more than he used to.' She paused. 'You don't have to worry about making excuses for him. I know what he's like. Just as long as he's treating you properly.'

'Everything's fine,' Isobel reassured her. 'He gave me the perfect wedding and the perfect honeymoon. And the flat's the sort of place where I only ever dreamed about living.'

'That isn't what I mean, and you know it.' As usual, Marcia was straight to the point. 'Is he making time for you?'

'Yes.' Not as much as she would've liked, but he spent time with her. And as for the baby question…it was still early days. At the age of thirty, she couldn't expect to fall pregnant immediately. She'd just have to be patient.

The 'man and a van' Alex had hired was there the next day to load up the boxes and take them to London. Alex had agreed to be there if the driver called him half an hour before arriving, but when Isobel got back to the flat Alex wasn't unpacking the boxes in the hallway as she'd expected him to be doing. And when she went up to the second floor she saw a small suitcase on their bed, almost packed.

'Alex? What's going on?' she asked.

'Something's come up,' he said. 'I have to go up to the Yorkshire coast for a couple of days—they've found what could be a Viking boat under a pub car park. The building work's stopped but I need to do some preliminary work to check out the extent of the site.' He gestured to the boxes. 'If you don't mind them staying there for the time being, I'll sort them out when I get back.'

'Alex, there's hardly room to get past them.' And if he was going to leave the boxes unpacked, why hadn't he put them upstairs in the spare bedroom rather than left them in the hallway?

'Sorry, Bel.' He raked a hand through his hair. 'I was going to start on them this afternoon, but then I got that phone call. You know what it's like. My job's to do the preliminary exploration—so I had a ton of things to set in motion, and I really have to go.' He gave her his most charming smile.

She'd just bet he'd practised that dishevelled, little-boy-lost look until he was perfect at it. She'd seen him use it before to get his own way. And it annoyed her that he was using it on her. She folded her arms. 'I see.'

'Look, if you want to unpack them yourself to get them out of the way, feel free. I don't have any secrets from you and I'm not possessive about my stuff.'

Alex wasn't possessive about anything.

'And how am I supposed to know what you want to keep and what you want to throw out?'

'Anything that duplicates whatever we already have—kitchen equipment and what have you—can go to a charity shop. You keep your books in the same order as mine, so if you wanted to merge our books on the shelves, that's fine by me. And I promise I'll sort out the remaining papers and anything you don't want to tackle as soon as I get back.'

'You're going *now*?'

'It makes sense. Otherwise I'll lose half a day's work tomorrow, travelling up to Yorkshire. And if I leave now it means I'll avoid the rush-hour traffic.'

And also, by her reckoning, he'd be there while it was still light enough for him to do a quick recce of the site. She was lucky he'd stayed in London long enough for her to get home before he left.

'I'm staying at the pub—it's just down the road from Whitby.' He flicked into his PDA, then scribbled down a number. 'That's the number, in case you need it.'

It was pointless being upset about it. She'd always known

that Alex's job came first. Yes, they were married—but it was a marriage of convenience and she'd better remember that. The only thing Alex had changed in his life was ditching the string of girlfriends. She believed him absolutely on that score, because Alex was always honest. 'Thanks. Need a hand with anything?'

'I'm practically done.' He kissed her lightly. 'Thanks, Bel. I knew you'd understand.'

He finished packing—incredibly swiftly, but then again she knew he was used to being on the move and travelling light— and then kissed her goodbye. 'I'll call you when I get there, OK?'

It wasn't OK, but she knew that look on his face. He was raring to go. Anything she said would fall on deaf ears. 'OK. Have a good trip.'

The door closed behind him, but she didn't go to the window to watch him walk down the path outside the flat. There was no point. Alex wouldn't think to look up and wave to her; his mind would be focused on the new site and the pos-sibilities.

The rest of the day stretched out before her. She didn't have anything better to do, she thought, so she might as well tackle the boxes. She unpacked Alex's books and spent a couple of hours rearranging the shelves in the study. Quite a few of his academic books were the same as hers; she flicked through to check and saw that Alex had done exactly what she'd done with her textbooks, so there were notes in the margins in his neat spiky handwriting. She didn't want to throw away her notes either or transfer them to a computer, so she ended up slotting his copies right next to hers.

He didn't have much music, only a few old CDs; again, she wasn't too surprised because Alex had been the first person she knew to get an MP3 player and transfer his music to a much more compact and portable form. There was even less kitchen stuff, because Alex never stayed long enough in one place to need to cook. But she dutifully boxed it up for him to take to the charity shop.

When she opened the next box, it was filled with files and loose papers; a quick scan along the spines told her that these were Alex's notes from his student days. She couldn't resist looking; after all, he'd given her carte blanche. As she'd expected, his undergraduate essays were well reasoned and fluent, and most of his marks were firsts or high upper seconds.

Then a piece of paper fell out of the file she was leafing through, one of the first from his doctoral studies.

Alex's illustrations were usually clear and precise, but this one wasn't of an artefact or a plan of a site or a cross-section. It was a sketch of a woman. A very pretty woman, though she looked a little older than the average student. Odd: Isobel had never known Alex to draw sketches of friends.

There were doodles on the same piece of paper, along with scrappy notes. It looked very much to her as if he'd been studying and let his mind wander to this woman. The initial 'D' appeared several times on the page with a heart drawn around it.

A lump rose in her throat and she wished she hadn't looked at the papers. Hadn't found this. Because even without that tell-tale initial, she knew that this was Dorinda. The woman who'd taught Alex not to trust or to believe in love. Alex had said he was over her—but he'd still kept her picture. So was he still carrying a torch for Dorinda?

As if on cue, the phone rang.

'Bel? I'm here. Well, I got here half an hour ago but I just had to go and take a look at the site first.'

Which was exactly what she'd known he'd do.

'It's incredible, Bel. You'd love it. I've taken some photographs and I'll email them to you tonight when I've downloaded them to my laptop. I wish you were here with me—why don't you call Rita and ask for some time off so you can come up here?'

'Alex, I can't let the museum down. I've already taken enough leave at short notice,' she reminded him. For their honeymoon—which already felt as if it had happened light years ago—and then moving house.

'I know and I'm sorry. I'm being selfish.' He sounded contrite. 'I just wanted to share this with you. Look, I'll be home soon. I'll call you tomorrow, OK?'

He clearly hadn't noticed that she'd been quieter than usual, Isobel thought as she replaced the receiver. Because, as usual, his head was full of his work.

She spent a while pottering round the flat. Even though she'd loved it from the moment she and Alex had viewed it, right at that moment she couldn't settle. She was cross with herself for mooching about, and even crosser with herself for missing Alex.

But the worst was the fact that she'd fallen in love with him. Made exactly the same mistake as she'd made with Gary: fallen for a man who'd never love her as much as she loved him.

Alex turned over for the umpteenth time and fluffed up his pillow. Even though he'd worked until late and his eyes were gritty and sore, he couldn't settle to sleep. And he knew why. Despite this being a single bed, it felt too big—because Isobel wasn't there. He'd become used to curling round her before drifting off to sleep, feeling the warmth of her body and the softness of her skin against him. Without her, it didn't feel right.

And he was feeling guilty about the way he'd packed without a second thought to come up here. OK, so it was part of his job—but he'd just left Isobel to it. Left her to unpack his stuff. Which made him a selfish bastard under anyone's terms.

She'd sounded slightly forlorn on the phone. Again, his fault. He'd uprooted her from the flat that had been her home since she'd split up with Gary. Steamrollered her into this marriage. Promised that he'd support her...and then left her to get on with it, alone.

He needed to make this better. So he'd buy her flowers on his way back to London—and, although he wasn't ready to say the words, he'd show her how he felt. How much she meant to him.

Just as soon as this project was over.

CHAPTER THIRTEEN

ALEX could see the light in the living room window as he climbed out of the car. Good. Isobel was definitely home, then. He took his suitcase, briefcase and the flowers from the back of the car, locked up, and headed for the flat.

'Bel?' he called as he unlocked the front door.

She appeared in the doorway to the living room. 'Hi. Did you have a good journey back?'

'Fine.' Better still because he knew he was coming home to her. Not that he was going to spook her by saying it. He'd already spooked himself enough. 'Have you eaten, yet?'

She shook her head. 'I thought I'd wait for you. I can order in a pizza if you're starving, otherwise dinner will be about half an hour.'

'Let's eat out.' He handed her the flowers. 'And these are for you. To say sorry. I shouldn't have left you to sort out all my stuff, Bel. It was thoughtless and not fair of me.'

'Thanks, but there was really no need to buy me flowers. I didn't mind sorting things out,' she said, but he thought her smile seemed slightly brittle. 'There's a box in the spare room that I've earmarked for the charity shop, so you just need to look through it and check I'm not getting rid of anything you want to keep. And I've left your notes for you to sort out. We really need another filing cabinet for the study, so I've ordered one.'

'Brilliant.' Trust her to see the problem and sort the solution without a fuss. 'Thanks, Bel. I appreciate it.'

'I'd better put these in water.'

Hmm. He'd expected at least a kiss hello. Was this just Isobel being her usual practical self and wanting to put the flowers in water before they started drooping, or was she avoiding him?

He wondered even more when she was quiet over dinner. Something was up. But what?

He found out later that night when he climbed into bed beside her and cuddled into her.

'Sorry. We can't tonight. It's my period.'

'OK. It's not a problem.'

Though it told him why she'd been a bit edgy that evening. Partly possible physical discomfort and partly the fact that it was proof of yet another month when they hadn't made a baby. Given what she'd told him before their wedding, she must be feeling thoroughly miserable right now. Disappointed. And hating herself for not being able to let go and relax.

The last thing he wanted to do was put pressure on her, make her feel bad about not being pregnant. On the other hand, Gary had kept her at arm's length because he hadn't wanted her to risk another miscarriage—which had made her feel even worse. This was a really, really difficult line to tread. It would be so easy to get it wrong. Whatever he did or said would risk hurting her.

So in the end he stayed where he was and kept his arms wrapped round her. 'Just so you know, I'm not trying to pressure you into having sex with me. I'm happy just to hold you tonight,' he said softly.

'Uh-huh.' But her body was tense, and she wasn't relaxing back against him the way she usually did.

'Would a back rub help?' he asked.

'No. Anyway, you've had a long drive. I ought to be the one offering you a back rub.'

'Hey. There are no "oughts" between us. No pressure, OK?'

'OK.'

He sighed. 'Bel.'

'What?'

'We agreed, no secrets. Spit it out.'

'I don't know what you're talking about.'

He switched on the light, then spun her round to face him. So he could see her eyes. 'You're not normally this quiet with me. Is it the baby thing that's upsetting you?'

She swallowed. 'No.'

In other words, yes, but she didn't want to admit it. 'Bel.' He stroked her face. 'We can go and see a specialist, if you want to. Just for a chat, maybe some initial tests. It might help put your mind at rest.'

'It's not that.'

'Then *tell* me. Unfortunately, mind-reading isn't one of my many talents.'

She shook her head. 'It's stupid.'

'Tell me anyway.' He kissed the tip of her nose. 'Better than bottling it up.'

She grimaced. 'All right. I was just checking what was in some of your files so I knew where to put them. And this sketch of Dorinda—at least, I assume it was her, as you'd doodled a "D" in a heart all over the page—fell out.'

'Sketch?' He frowned. 'Blimey. They must have been really old files—I haven't looked at my doctorate stuff in years. And it must've been on the back of some notes I wanted at the time or I would probably have thrown it out.'

'Oh.' She flushed, looking embarrassed.

'Isobel, you don't seriously think I'm still holding a torch for her, do you? I haven't seen her for years and I don't have the slightest interest in where she is or what she's doing now. And besides, I'm married to *you*.' He pulled her into his arms. 'Bel, I'm not Gary.'

'I know.'

'Then give me a cuddle instead of the silent treatment.'

He almost—almost—told her that he'd missed her. That he was glad to be home. That all hadn't felt quite right with his world when he was away from her.

But this wasn't part of the deal.

And they'd both been burned by love before. It was better to keep it the way it was. So he kept his thoughts to himself, and just held her until they both drifted into sleep.

Two more months passed and Isobel's period was regular as clockwork, practically down to the hour. And every time it happened, she bawled her eyes out and then splashed her eyes with water so Alex wouldn't notice when he got home.

Every time they made love, Isobel found herself wishing afterwards that this had been the right time, that they'd made a baby—and every time she hated herself for being so needy, for not being able to emulate his ability to take life as it came. She should be making love with him because she wanted *him*, not because they were trying to make a baby.

She'd even thought about buying an ovulation kit to help them pinpoint the right window for having sex—but then again, she and Alex were having sex regularly. Plenty of it.

So the problem was obviously with her.

Alex had mentioned going to see a specialist, but when she hadn't immediately leapt at the idea he hadn't mentioned it again. He was busy at work and he just didn't seem to have noticed that time was ticking away and they still hadn't made a baby. Or maybe he had noticed that she still wasn't pregnant—and the fact he hadn't brought it up with her meant that he was secretly relieved at not being a father. His job wasn't exactly conducive to fatherhood, was it?

She wrapped her arms round herself. How stupid could she be? He'd told her right from the start that he didn't believe in love. That their relationship was a deep friendship plus great sex. She knew his job was his life. So how on earth had she let herself get to the point where she was wishing he'd put her before his job?

She dragged in a breath.

She knew how she'd done it.

By falling in love with him.

So much for going into this with her eyes wide open. She'd kidded herself that her feelings for Alex were just friendship. Told herself that when he was away and the bed felt too wide, it was simply because she'd grown used to him being there, that it was a habit.

It was nothing of the kind.

She was in love with her husband.

A husband who didn't love her and never would, because he wouldn't ever let himself be that vulnerable again.

How stupid could she be?

She tried taking a leaf out of Alex's book and losing herself in her job, but it just didn't feel the same any more. Every time she did her Roman domestic life exhibition at the museum and saw mothers in the audience carrying their babies around in slings and holding the hand of an older child, she had to bite back the envy.

Another month went by. Isobel had always thought wryly that she could set her watch by her period—practically know the second she'd need to take a coffee break on every fourth Thursday.

So when it reached Thursday lunchtime, she found herself wondering.

The sensible side of her knew that it couldn't be. The stress of wanting a baby and still not falling pregnant had probably thrown her cycle for a loop.

But all the same, hope fluttered in her stomach.

When it was time to leave for the day and her period still hadn't started, the flutter turned into a herd of elephants stomping about in her stomach. She had to know the truth.

There was only one way to find out. She called into the supermarket and bought a test kit on the way home. And she sat in the kitchen with the test kit on the scrubbed pine table before her.

To test, or not to test?

Even though she'd tried to be brave about it, she knew that a false alarm would rip her heart out.

But if she was pregnant, what then? How would Alex react? Right at that moment she couldn't second-guess him.

And what if she miscarried again? That was the point where her last marriage fell apart. Would it be the same with Alex? Although she knew intellectually that Alex was nothing like Gary, she couldn't shift the fear.

'Enough,' she said out loud. 'Calm down. Deep breaths. This isn't *you*, Isobel,' she told herself. 'Stop panicking. Like Alex's grandmother would say, you're building bridges to trouble and that's not good.'

What she really should do was take it step by step. Do the test. And once she knew one way or another, she could take the next step.

She went into the bathroom. The last time she remembered feeling this sick was when a mutual friend told her the news—

that Gary's new love had had a baby. The baby she'd wanted so much herself.

But it wasn't Gary's baby she wanted. It was Alex's. A child with those same amazing eyes and carefree smile and dark curls.

She did the test, and waited. The seconds felt as if they were dragging.

Please, please, please let it be positive, she prayed silently. Please let her have Alex's baby. She really didn't mind if it was a girl or a boy; she just wanted a child to share the world with.

She looked at the clock. How could time move so slowly? Surely it was against the laws of physics?

'Please let it be positive. Please. Is it so much to ask?' she whispered.

Another glance at the clock. Five seconds.

She looked at the test kit. There was a blue line in one of the windows, telling her that the test was working.

She closed her eyes again. Please be positive. *Please* be positive, she willed.

Again, she looked at the clock. Surely it was time, now. Heart thumping, she looked at the test stick and burst into tears—noisy, hot, shuddering sobs. 'Thank you God, fate, whoever's in charge of the universe—thank you,' she whispered when her sobs finally died away.

She checked the test again, just to be sure she hadn't misread it and it hadn't changed; then she bathed her eyes, the cool water soothing her hot, swollen skin.

Pregnant.

She was definitely pregnant

She rested one palm against her abdomen. 'Hang on in there, little one. Everything's going to be just fine now,' she said.

So. Step one. She was definitely pregnant.

Now she had to tell Alex.

She was tempted to ring him, but if he was still in a meeting, it wasn't fair to interrupt him. A text, on the other hand, was something he could pick up at his convenience.

She tapped the message into her phone.

Any idea when you'll be home?

To her surprise, he replied almost instantly.

Hour or so. Why, want to go out for dinner?

She couldn't tell him news like this by text.

No. Just wanted to talk to you.

A few moments later, her phone rang. 'Bel? What's the matter?'

'Nothing.'

'I have three sisters, remember,' Alex said. 'I know that "nothing" doesn't mean anything of the kind. What's wrong?'

'I don't really want to talk about it on the phone.' She wanted to tell him face to face. Where, very briefly, he wouldn't be able to mask his first reaction. She needed to know how he felt about this.

'Do you need me home now?' He sounded concerned rather than irritated.

'No.' *Yes.* 'I'm fine,' she reassured him, knowing she was taking a slight licence with the truth. 'There's nothing to worry about.' That much at least was true. 'See you when you get home.'

'OK, honey. See you soon.'

* * *

It wasn't like Isobel to bother him at work.

Though he had been putting in a lot of hours at work lately. Neglecting her.

Alex made a rough calculation in his head. Hell. Her period had probably just started and she was feeling miserable. And this particular piece of work wasn't desperately urgent. Right now, she probably needed a hug more than he needed to do this. He could catch up later.

He saved the file, locked the office behind him and stopped off for supplies on the way home. Armed with tissues and three large bars of good chocolate, he walked indoors.

'Bel? I'm home.'

She emerged from the kitchen. 'You didn't have to come straight back.'

He took one look at her and knew he'd made the right decision. 'Yes, I did.' He dropped the plastic bag on the floor and enfolded her in his arms. 'You've been crying. Your eyes are all puffy. What's wrong?'

'I...' She dragged in a breath. 'I'm being stupid.'

He could feel wetness seeping through his shirt. 'Don't cry, honey. We'll work something out. Look, I'm not putting any pressure on you here, but maybe it's time we went to see someone about this. We'll get some tests run—on *both* of us,' he emphasised, 'and see what's going on and what our options are.'

'My period hasn't started, Alex.'

'We can try again next month. Maybe we'll go away for a weekend. Somewhere we can both relax and unwind. Take the stress off, and maybe it'll happen.'

'I said,' she repeated, 'my period hasn't started.'

Her words finally sank in and he drew back slightly. So if it wasn't her period... 'Then what is it? Your parents are all right?'

'They're fine. I...um...come and sit down.'

There was a weird sensation flickering down his spine. It took Alex a while to identify it as fear.

Was she telling him this was all over? That she'd met someone else?

He let her lead him into the kitchen and sat down at the table. 'Bel? Talk to me. What's going on?'

'I'm not sure how to say this.'

The flickering grew stronger. 'Whatever it is, I'd prefer you to tell me straight.' Actually, that wasn't true. If she was about to tell him it was over, he didn't want to hear it at all. And that scared him even more: since when had Isobel become this important to him?

She handed him something that felt like a flattened pencil wrapped in a tissue. 'Take a look at this.'

He frowned, and unwrapped it as she went to the opposite end of the table and leaned against it.

And then he realised she'd given him a pregnancy test. He'd never actually seen one before; he'd never been in a position to need to see one before. And he really wasn't quite sure what he was looking at. 'Are you telling me…?'

She nodded. 'I'm late. And I'm always, *always* on time. Practically to the hour.' She swallowed hard. 'I thought I might be late because I was…well, a bit tense.'

Completely stressed out, more like. And he'd been too wrapped up in his new job to notice just how bad she'd been feeling. Guilt made the back of his neck feel hot.

'But I needed to know for sure,' she continued. 'So I bought a test. And, um, it's positive.'

He stared at the test stick and then at her, stunned. 'You're pregnant.'

'Yes.'

She looked worried sick and it was hardly surprising. She'd had two miscarriages, and Gary hadn't exactly been supportive afterwards. She was probably panicking that this pregnancy wouldn't last, either—and that he'd let her down the way Gary had.

Or was she worrying that he'd changed his mind about his promise to her, that he didn't want this baby after all?

Of course he hadn't changed his mind.

But he needed to get his head round what she'd just told him.

Although intellectually he'd expected this to happen eventually, he hadn't been prepared for it emotionally. Hadn't known how he'd feel when she finally told him they were having a baby.

He blinked. 'We're having a baby.'

'Yes.'

'I'm going to be a dad.' There was a lump in his throat a mile wide and a weird sensation in his chest that he couldn't explain. 'Oh, Bel. We're having a baby.'

'You're OK about that?'

He pushed his chair back, walked over to her and wrapped his arms round her. 'More than OK.' That vision he'd had of a little girl like Isobel... It might just be coming true. 'But you shouldn't be on your feet. Sit down.'

'I don't need to—' she began.

He solved her protest by dragging another chair out, sitting down and pulling her onto his lap. 'Bel. I'm so...' He shook his head. 'I can't find the words. It's as if someone's knocked everything I knew out of my head. But it's a good feeling.'

'I thought you might...well...'

'Back out of it? Want to change my mind?' He saw the tear start to slide down her cheek, and kissed it away. 'No. Don't cry, Bel. It's all going to be just fine.'

'I think I'm crying because I'm happy. And I'm so relieved. I thought there was something wrong—'

He placed his finger gently on her lips. 'Shh. Nothing's

wrong. I know we've had to wait a bit, but it'll be worth the wait.' He smiled. 'So do you want to tell your mum first or mine?'

She shook her head. 'Not until twelve weeks. I don't want to tell anyone. Just in case.'

Although she didn't say it, he could read the fear in her eyes. She was terrified that she was going to miscarry again. How far gone had she been when she'd lost her last baby? He hadn't asked her—and now most definitely wasn't the right time to pose the question. 'Try not to worry,' he said, stroking her face. 'The odds are on our side. The chances are that everything's going to be absolutely fine, this time. But you don't take any risks or lift anything heavier than a tissue.'

She coughed. 'That's a bit over the top, Alex.'

'All right. Nothing heavier than a book, then,' he amended. 'And as from now, you're off all housework duties. I'll do them.'

'You're never here,' she pointed out.

He brushed it aside. 'We'll get a cleaner. I loathe ironing so we'll use a laundry service. And—'

'Alex, I'm pregnant, not sick.'

'You're pregnant. And you've had a rough time in the past. So I'm not taking any chances with you.' He took a risk and told her straight. 'You're too important to me.'

Her eyes filled with tears again. 'I'm sorry. I'm being wet.'

'No, you're not. It's just hormones.' He smiled. 'Saskia used to ring me and weep down the phone when she was pregnant. The only way to shut her up was to have chocolate delivered every three days. And then she used to ring me up and cry because I was being nice to her.'

As he'd hoped, the ridiculous story made her smile. 'Alex, you're completely mad.'

'The word you were looking for is "eccentric",' he corrected, and kissed her lightly. 'We're going to have a baby. And I'm going to take care of you, I promise.'

CHAPTER FOURTEEN

IF ANYONE had told Isobel that Alex would start coming home from work at a reasonable time and his bedtime reading would involve a pile of books about pregnancy and babies instead of obscure texts and archaeological journals, she would've laughed.

But he did.

He also insisted on taking over the kitchen while she sat with her feet up. Although he was a great cook, it drove her crazy, having to sit still and do nothing.

When he brought her a glass of water and a multi-vitamin tablet formulated especially for pregnant women, she'd had enough.

'Alex, you're steamrollering me again, like you did over the wedding. I know you're trying to help and be a new man or what have you, but I'm quite capable of looking after myself.'

'Agreed, but all the books say women find strong smells hard to cope with in the early weeks of pregnancy, so you're better off out of the kitchen. And I'm cooking things with as little scent as possible so the kitchen smells don't make you feel sick.'

'I'm not getting morning sickness at the moment. Anyway, you hate bland food.'

He shrugged. 'It's only for a few months. I can put up with it, as long as you're all right.'

Alex was trying his hardest to be domesticated, for her sake. So he really, really cared about her. He might not say the L-word, and he might still say he didn't believe in it, but the way he was acting told her that he cared.

And Isobel had to blink back tears—tears she was glad Alex hadn't noticed, or she would've had to claim they were due to her hormones being all over the place. She just wanted him to learn to trust her. To learn that it was safe to love her—that he could give her his heart and she'd treasure it. That she'd love him all the way back.

To Isobel's mingled shock and pleasure, Alex actually took time off to go take her for the booking-in appointment with the midwife—and he held her hand all the way, including in the waiting room. And he held her hand even more tightly when she explained to the midwife about her previous two miscarriages.

'Normally, my advice is that gentle sexual intercourse is fine in pregnancy—but in this case I'd suggest avoiding intercourse for the first three months,' the midwife advised. 'But there are other things you can do—relax together, massage each other, have a candlelit bath together.'

'Isobel and the baby come first,' Alex said immediately. 'I don't want to take any risks.'

The midwife nodded. 'That's good. Having previous miscarriages doesn't mean you can't carry a baby to term, Isobel, but I would like to see you a bit more frequently so I can keep an eye on you. And if you're feeling worried at all, even if it's something you think is silly, just call me or one of the other midwives on your team—that's what we're here for. Now, I'll book you in for a dating scan, and you'll get a letter with the appointment later in the week—probably for two or three weeks' time.'

When the appointment came through, Alex checked his

diary and made a noise of frustration. 'I'm supposed to be in Chester then—and for the two days before the scan, too. I'll get them to reschedule.'

'What if they can't?' Isobel asked.

'They'll have to, if they want me there. Because no way in hell am I going to miss our first scan.'

While Alex was away, he called Isobel every day. He nagged her like crazy about putting her feet up and getting lots of rest. And when he'd been passing a shopping centre, he'd been unable to resist going into a toyshop and buying the softest, softest teddy bear.

Their baby's first present.

Isobel had been adamant that she wouldn't even look at baby clothes or nursery furniture or a baby book until after the twelfth week, but surely one little bear wouldn't hurt? He'd sneak it into a drawer until she was ready to talk about buying things for the baby.

Isobel was curled up on the sofa, reading, when she felt a familiar dragging sensation in her abdomen.

No.

She froze.

It couldn't be.

Please, don't let it be that.

She forced herself to take a deep breath in. And out. And in. And out. Stay calm, for the baby's sake, even though panic was galloping along every nerve-end.

Gingerly, she walked to the bathroom. Saw the blood.

OK. Maybe it was just spotting. Plenty of women had spotting in early pregnancy.

But she'd been here before. She knew this was too heavy to be just spotting.

She was losing her baby.

Along with her dreams.

Shaking, she called Alex's mobile.

'The cell phone that you are calling is unavailable,' the automated message told her. 'Please try later.'

But later would be too late. She needed him here right now.

It looked as if she was going to have to deal with this on her own. She took a deep breath and called the number her midwife had given her. To her relief, it was Jenny, the midwife who'd seen her at the clinic.

'I'm bleeding,' she whispered.

'All right, love. I know you're worried, but I'll be with you as soon as I can. Just lie on the sofa with your feet up, try to relax and try not to worry. Is anyone with you?'

'No. Alex is away on business.'

'Is there anyone you can call to be with you?'

'My parents are a good couple of hours away.'

'What about friends?'

Isobel took a deep breath. 'We haven't told anyone yet. I—I wanted to wait until I was twelve weeks. Just in case.'

'I'll be there as soon as possible, love.' Jenny double-checked her address. 'Try not to worry. Spotting's very common in early pregnancy—and your hormones will still be all over the place, so if this is around the time when you would normally have had a period, it could just be that.'

'It could be,' Isobel said, trying for bravery. Though she knew this feeling all too well. It wasn't just hormones or spotting.

When Jenny arrived, she examined Isobel very gently, then stroked her hand. 'Isobel, love, we need to get you to hospital.'

'I'm losing my baby.' It wasn't a question. She knew.

'It might be a threatened miscarriage. They'll be able to

tell in the hospital with the scanner—and if that's the case, we'll put you on bedrest for a while and keep monitoring you until the scare's over.'

'Bedrest? But...'

'You're on your own. I know.' Jenny squeezed her hand. 'Don't worry, I'll go with you. Have you managed to get in touch with Alex yet?'

'No.'

'We'll try again in a minute. I'll just call you in.' She glanced at her watch. 'And I'll drive you in myself. It'll be quicker.' Jenny rang the hospital, but Isobel didn't have a clue what the midwife was saying. She was too busy holding onto the tiny fragment of hope that it was a threatened miscarriage. That, this time, her baby would hold on.

'Let's go,' Jenny said softly.

'What if one of your other patients needs you?'

'I'm supposed to be off duty in about three minutes,' Jenny said with a smile. 'So they'll be able to talk to whoever's on the roster.'

Isobel bit her lip. 'I can't ask you to go to the hospital with me in your time off.'

'You haven't asked me. I'm insisting.'

The midwife's kindness made Isobel want to cry. But she was terrified that if she started, she'd never stop. So she forced herself to smile. 'Thank you.'

'Alex and Bel can't take your call right now. Please leave a message after the beep.'

Alex frowned. Isobel hadn't said anything about being out tonight. Not that he was a control freak—just that he wanted to be sure she was all right. From what he'd heard, most new fathers-to-be were a bit overprotective about their pregnant partners. But he was doubly so because of Isobel's past.

Coming here on this job had been wrong. He should've called in some favours and got someone else to do the exploration. Right now Isobel was vulnerable and it had been a bad idea to leave her on her own.

But maybe her friends at work had suggested an evening out. A meal after work, or an impromptu visit to the cinema. Isobel was too sensible to take any risks, he knew. She'd pace herself, and take a taxi rather than the tube if she felt tired. And she'd probably tried to call him earlier to let him know she was out; the mobile phone reception around here was atrocious, and he'd had to wait until he was back at the hotel and could use the phone in his room to call her.

He didn't bother leaving a message on their home phone; instead, he called her mobile.

'The cell phone you are calling is switched off. Please try later or send a text.'

Definitely the cinema, then. OK. He'd call her again after dinner.

On the way to the hospital, the cramps grew worse. On Jenny's insistence, Isobel had kept trying to call Alex, but still there was no reply. 'He's in an area with poor reception,' she told Jenny.

'We'll try again in a bit. Let's go up to the ward. The sonographer might not say anything at first as he tries to find the baby, but don't worry about that,' Jenny reassured her. 'It's perfectly normal.'

As they went through the doors of the ward, Isobel could see her name written on the white board, under the heading 'emergency'.

Emergency.

There was nothing normal about that.

But it didn't send Isobel into screaming panic. Right at that moment she couldn't feel anything.

She let herself be led into the little cubicle, lay on the bed and bared her abdomen for the radioconductive gel. All the while, Jenny was holding her hand and talking to her, but Isobel couldn't take in a single word.

And then she saw the pity in the doctor's face.

'I'm so sorry, Mrs Richardson. There isn't a heartbeat. I'm afraid you've miscarried,' the doctor said gently.

Everything after that just blurred.

How was she going to tell Alex?

'Mrs Richardson?'

'I'm sorry. I…' She dragged in a breath. Now wasn't the time to go to pieces.

'No need to apologise. It's a very difficult thing to have to take in.' The doctor sat next to her. 'You're about nine weeks, according to your notes, so I'd recommend that we just let nature take its course rather than bring you in for a D and C. Do you have anyone who can be with you for the next few days?'

'My husband's away on business.'

'If you'd rather stay in overnight, we can arrange that.'

Cold, clinical hospital. So unlike the bright, sunny nursery she'd allowed herself to plan in her head. But it made no difference. Her baby wasn't going to be there. 'I'd rather go home, please.'

'I'll take you,' Jenny said softly. 'And I can talk you through what to expect.'

Isobel shrugged. 'Same as last time, I presume.'

'I'm so sorry, love.' Jenny squeezed her hand. 'Do you want to wait here for a while?'

Isobel shook her head. 'I'd just like to go home, please.'

She managed to hold herself together on the way back to the flat, mainly because she knew that if she started crying she wouldn't be able to stop.

'Would you like me to ring Alex for you?' Jenny asked.

'No, it's fine. You've done so much for me already this evening, and it's not fair to expect you to stay,'

'I'll wait with you until you manage to get through to him.'

Isobel gave her a tired smile. 'I'll be all right, Jenny. I was half expecting this to happen, anyway. But thank you for being so kind.'

The midwife still looked concerned. 'I'd rather not leave you.'

Isobel patted her hand. 'Honestly, I'll be fine. Thank you.'

She kept the smile on her face until the door closed behind her.

And then she walked into the bathroom, stripped off her clothes, and stood under the shower. Slid down the wall until she was sitting on the floor with the water trickling down over her, her knees up to her chin and her head resting on her knees. Even though the water was warm, she felt as if she'd never be warm again. And she was so, so empty.

She stayed there until the water ran cold, and then dragged herself out of the shower. Wrapped herself in a towel. Went through all the mechanical steps of sorting out clean clothes and a sanitary towel.

White.

The colour of mourning, in some cultures.

But she felt too cold, too empty, to mourn.

She had no idea how much time passed until the phone rang. She answered it mechanically.

'Bel? You're back, then.'

'Back?'

'I rang earlier. There was no answer, so I assumed you were out with people from work. You didn't answer your mobile, either.'

Her tongue felt as if it had stuck to the roof of her mouth. 'No. I must've been in the shower and didn't hear the phone.' It was a complete lie, but to her relief he didn't question her.

'Are you OK?'

No.

Far from it.

And right then she felt that nothing would ever be OK again.

'Just tired.'

That was true. She was tired to the depth of her soul. But if she told him what had really happened tonight, he'd drive straight home. She couldn't do that to him. Knowing Alex, he would've been working since early morning, probably until just before he called her. A four-hour drive on top of that would be unfair. And if he ended up falling asleep at the wheel...

No.

She'd lost their baby.

She couldn't bear to lose Alex, too.

He was speaking again.

'Sorry, Alex. I didn't catch that.'

'I'll be home in two days. Then on Friday morning we've got the scan.'

Not any more. She dug her nails into her palm to stop herself crying. 'I know.' She was trying so hard, but she knew she didn't sound as excited as she should be.

'Are you sure you're all right?'

She could practically hear the frown in his voice. 'Just tired,' she said again.

'Go and have a warm bath and then an early night,' he said. 'Sweet dreams. And I'll call you tomorrow.'

'Goodnight,' she said, still just about in control.

And when she replaced the receiver, she curled up into a ball. Please, somehow, let her get through the next day.

CHAPTER FIFTEEN

WHEN Alex called the following evening, something about Isobel's voice didn't sound quite right. 'Bel, is anything wrong?' he asked

'Why would there be?'

'It's just…' A feeling that something wasn't as it should be. But he couldn't put his finger on it. 'How was your day?'

'Routine. How was yours?'

'Good. I did some geophysics tests today and I think we've got something very interesting.'

It wasn't until he'd said goodbye and put the phone down that he realised what was odd.

Isobel hadn't mentioned the baby or the scan.

Given that the scan meant they'd be seeing their baby on the screen, that it would help her believe she really was pregnant and it really was going to work out, this time, he'd expected her to be all bubbly and happy and hardly able to wait. To be planning how to tell their family, how many copies of the scan photo they'd need.

The more he thought about it, the more he was sure that something was very, very wrong.

She'd answered his questions either with another question or with some anodyne response. So clearly something had happened and she was trying not to tell him because he was miles away and she didn't want him to worry.

Time to call in some favours.

Two phone calls netted him the result he wanted. And then he threw everything into his suitcase, loaded that and his briefcase into his car, settled his hotel bill and drove back to London, not caring that it was late and it would take him four hours to get home and he'd arrive at stupid o'clock, while Isobel was fast asleep. Right now, he had a feeling that she needed him. And he intended to be there for her.

When he arrived back in London, he let himself quietly into the flat and left his luggage in the hallway. He tiptoed up the stairs, and stripped off outside their bedroom so the noise wouldn't wake her. He padded across the carpet to their bed and slid under the duvet beside her, trying not to disturb her. He'd talk to her tomorrow, find out what was wrong then. But for tonight he was happy just to sleep with his wife in his arms.

Although Isobel stirred when he curled his body round hers, she stayed asleep. Alex just held her close, and was asleep himself only a couple of minutes later.

When the alarm shrilled, Alex groaned and reached out to hit the snooze button.

'Alex? When did you get back?' Isobel asked.

'Last night,' he mumbled, not opening his eyes. 'Shh. Go back to sleep. Five more minutes.'

But she'd gone rigid in his arms. Sighing inwardly, he opened his eyes and sat up. 'Good morn—' He stopped abruptly. She looked absolutely terrible. Her face was white and there were shadows under her eyes. But what really shocked him was the way the light had disappeared from her eyes. 'Bel? What's happened?'

'I lost the baby.' Her voice was flat, unemotional.

He stared at her, unable to take it in at first. She'd lost their baby? When?

And then he realised.

'When I called, the night before last. When you were out.'

'Yes.' There was no tone whatsoever in her voice.

'Why the *hell* didn't you tell me?'

She shrugged. 'Apart from the fact you were a four-hour drive away and it wasn't fair to drag you back, it had already happened. There was nothing you could have done.'

'Yes, I could. I could've been there to hold your hand and support you through it.' He shook his head in disbelief. 'Oh, Bel.' He went to put his arms round her, hold her close, but she moved out of reach.

'Don't. I'm OK.'

No, she wasn't. She was very far from it. She looked and sounded so brittle that she'd shatter at any moment. 'Bel.' He raked a hand through his hair. 'I don't know what to say. Except I'm so, so sorry.'

She shrugged. 'It's not your fault.'

'It's not *yours*, either.' He paused. 'If you'd told me, I would've come straight home.'

'Driving for four hours after a long day's work?'

'It's what I did last night,' he pointed out. 'Bel, you didn't sound yourself. I *knew* something was wrong.'

'Well, now you know.'

'And I came straight back.' He reached out to take her hand. 'Don't shut me out, Bel.'

'I'm fine. I need to get ready for work.'

'You're not fine, Bel. And you're in no fit state to go to work.'

When she ignored him and started to climb out of the bed, he moved, wrapping his arms round her and hauling her onto his lap.

'What are you doing?' she snapped.

'Holding you. Because you're not going *anywhere*,' he said, keeping his arms tightly round her. 'Honey, if you put a brave face on it and go to work, you're going to end up in meltdown.'

'I'll be fine.'

Like hell, she would. He refused to let her go. 'Bel, I know you're hurting—and if it's any consolation, I'm hurting, too.'

'Are you?'

It shocked him that she could even question that. Didn't she know? 'How can you think otherwise?'

'You said...' She swallowed hard. 'You said we'd see how things went.'

'Which doesn't mean I was indifferent. You'd told me what happened with Gary, and I didn't want to pile any more pressure on you. I wanted our baby, Isobel. Every bit as much as you did. OK, I admit, before we had that conversation I'd never really thought about having children—but when you showed me that pregnancy test and I realised we were really going to have a baby, it was... I can't explain it.' He shook his head. 'It was as if I'd been let out of a locked room, a room I'd never even realised I was trapped in until I was let out. And then suddenly this whole new world was around me. A world I could share with you and our child. And I was so happy about it, Bel.' He paused. 'Though right now I'm feeling guilty.'

She stared at him. 'Why?'

'Because I should've been here to take care of you.'

She shook her head. 'It wouldn't have made any difference. You couldn't have stopped it happening.'

'But I would've been here with you when it happened— you wouldn't have had to go through this all on your own.' He stroked her face. 'And even though you know I don't believe in superstitions...' He knew that she did. She'd been worried about seeing him on the day of their wedding. And she'd be so upset when she found out what he'd done. But he couldn't lie to her about this. 'Promise you won't hate me for this, Bel?'

'Hate you for what?'

'I know you said you didn't want to tell anyone until twelve weeks. And I didn't tell anyone—I said I had important personal stuff to do on Friday but I didn't say what it was.' He closed his eyes. 'But I bought something. For our baby. I wanted to…' Suddenly he couldn't go on. He buried his head in his shoulder, inhaling her scent. Needing her warmth. Hoping that she'd somehow manage to find more strength in him than he could right at that minute.

'Alex?'

At last her arms were round him and she was holding him back. But it made him choke. He didn't deserve this.

'Alex, you're scaring me.'

He lifted his head. 'I…I bought a teddy bear. I wanted to buy our baby's first toy.' He dragged in a breath. 'I'm sorry. I shouldn't have done it. I shouldn't have tempted fate.'

'You buying a teddy didn't make me lose—lose…' She stared at him, and a tear rolled down her face. Her mouth was working, but no sounds were coming out.

He kept his arms wrapped tightly round her. 'I'm here, Bel. And I know right now this feels like the end of the world…' he rocked her gently, feeling the tears start to slide down his own face '…but it isn't. We'll get through this, I promise. Because we've still got each other. And that's not going to change.'

She buried her head in his shoulder and sobbed her heart out. He held her close, feeling her pain as well as his own.

Eventually she stopped shaking and pulled back from him slightly. 'Alex. I understand if you want to walk away.' Her voice was thick with tears.

Walk away? He didn't understand. 'Why would I walk away?'

'Because I...because I lost our baby.'

He brushed his mouth lightly against hers. 'I'm not Gary, Bel. I'm not going to walk out on you.'

'But I might not be able to have children, Alex. And I can't do that to you.' She dragged in a breath. 'I can't take your choices away.'

'You're not taking my choices away.'

'But you just said you wanted a child.'

'I do. With *you*.' He stroked her face. 'If it turns out we can't have a biological child of our own, there are other ways. Adoption, fostering...we'll still have options.'

'You'd be better off finding someone else. Someone who can give you a family.'

'I'm not Gary, Bel,' he repeated. 'And here's the kicker. I don't want anyone else. I just want you. And I think I always have.'

She stared at him. 'I don't understand.'

'You've always been the one I've talked to.'

'Because we're friends.'

'You're more than that to me,' he said softly. 'And the more I think about it, the more I realise I didn't really love Dorinda all those years ago. I was in lust with her, yes, but I couldn't talk to her—not the way I talk to you. And I didn't tell you about her at the time because...' He shrugged. 'I suppose I was ashamed. I'd been really, really naïve and stupid, and I didn't want you to think badly of me.'

'I've never thought badly of you, Alex.'

'You're the centre of my life, Bel. You have been for a long while. I wouldn't admit it to myself, but when you got married it meant that you were off limits. And I realise now I dated so much because I was searching for someone who'd have

that same special relationship with me that you had. Except
none of them matched up to you.'

'But…' she shook her head in seeming disbelief '…Alex,
I'm ordinary and the women you dated were stunning.'

He stroked her face. 'Number one, Isobel Richardson,
you're very far from ordinary. And number two, they might
have been physically gorgeous, but they didn't have that
certain something about them. There's only one woman like
that as far as I'm concerned.' He held her gaze. 'I know my
timing's lousy—and saying this is against all my principles—
but I need you to know, Bel. I love you. Like nobody else I've
ever known.'

'You love me?'

He nodded. 'So there's my other guilty confession. I love
you. I adore my job, but I hate being away from you. I miss
you like hell when I'm away. And I know I steamrollered you
into this marriage and I haven't looked after you properly, but
if you'll give me a second chance I swear I'll be the best
husband. I'll put you first.'

'You love me,' she repeated, her voice full of wonder.

'Yeah.' He smiled wryly. 'I love you.'

'Alex.' She swallowed hard. 'I thought you'd never let me
close. That you'd never trust me enough to let me love you.'

'I trust you with my life, Bel.' He brushed his mouth
against hers. 'You *are* my life.'

She shook her head. 'That's not true. Your job comes first.'

'Not any more. And I'll prove it.'

'How?'

'Take off your wedding ring.'

Isobel froze. Why did he want her to take off the ring? Had
she misheard what he said earlier? Was he saying that their
marriage was over, after all? 'What?'

'Take off your wedding ring,' he repeated. 'I need to show you something.'

She frowned, but did so. He held out his palm, and she dropped the ring into it. He did something clever, and then suddenly the ring fanned out into three hoops.

'It's a gimmel ring,' she said in surprise. Why on earth hadn't she guessed? She'd even remarked on how pretty it was, the sandwich of white gold between yellow. And she'd seen medieval gimmel rings at the museum: interlocking rings that joined into one, symbolising the joining of two lives. There was often a secret message engraved on the middle hoop. She should've realised that Alex wouldn't give her just a normal ring.

'Take a look,' he said.

Engraved on the middle hoop were the initials AT and IA. His and hers. And in between was engraved the date of their wedding.

'Turn it over,' he said softly.

There was a second engraving. *Semper.*

Latin for 'always'.

'Alex…'

'Just so you know I'm not flannelling you now. I guess I've always known I love you,' he said. 'I told myself you were a just good friend. Someone I've always been comfortable with, and the amazing sex was a bonus. But if I'm honest you're the only woman I've ever told my dreams to. And although I told you at the time it was a marriage of convenience—a way of making sure I got the job and staying around a bit more for Mum's sake—I knew in my heart that it was more than that. I meant what I said in my wedding vows.'

'You didn't say anything about love.'

'Because I was still pretty much in denial. But I'm not any more. I love you, Isobel. So very much. And if you can't love me back, it doesn't really matter, because I love you enough for both of us.' He swallowed hard. 'I guess what I'm trying to say is that I'd rather be with you than without you.'

She dragged in a breath. 'I love you, too, Alex,' she whispered. 'If I'm honest about it, I've loved you for years. Ever since you kissed me when I was eighteen. But you always had this string of girlfriends and you never even seemed to notice I was female. So I settled for second-best—being your friend.' She smiled wryly. 'It's one of the reasons why I didn't want to marry you. I'd already been through a marriage where my husband didn't love me. Marrying someone who was up front about the fact that he didn't believe in love… It was going to be a recipe for disaster.'

'Our marriage isn't a disaster. And I do love you,' Alex said. 'Right now we've hit a rough patch—but that's in our life, not our marriage. We'll get through this. *Together*.'

'I wanted our baby so much, Alex.'

'I know, honey.' He drew her close again. 'So did I.'

'All the months of hoping and being disappointed, and then finding I was pregnant and being so scared in case something went wrong…and now it has.' She closed her eyes. 'So much for third time lucky.'

He stroked her hair. 'There's a glass-half-full side to this.'

'How?' How could he possibly see something positive in this, when their world had just fallen apart?

'You said that the doctors wouldn't investigate until after three miscarriages. Now,' he said gently, 'they'll be able to help us. We can have tests, find out why it happened. Find out what our options are.'

Fear flooded through her. 'Supposing we can't have children at all?'

'We'll face that if and when we come to it.' He stroked her face. 'First steps, first. I'll ring the doctor this morning and make an appointment. It might not be easy and it might take a while, but we can lean on each other. Together we're strong.' He kissed her lightly. 'Go have a shower. Though you're not going to work today. I'll talk to your boss—because Rita really needs to know about this, Bel. And it's going to be easier on you if I tell her.'

She shook her head. 'Alex, I can't ask you to do that.'

'You're not asking. I'm offering.' He stroked her face. 'Actually, no. I'm being bossy. But I'm doing it for the right reasons—I'm trying to protect you from being hurt.'

She hugged him. 'Thank you,' she said softly. 'Because I don't think I can tell anyone without bawling my eyes out.'

'Go and have that shower,' she said.

She did so. When she'd got dressed she padded downstairs to the kitchen, her wet hair still wrapped in a towel. Alex was sitting at the kitchen table, a mug of coffee in one hand and the phone in the other, clearly listening to someone talking on the other end of the line. He looked up, saw her and nodded to the cafetière. It's fresh, he mouthed.

'Uh-huh. Right. Thanks a lot. I'll call you next week,' he said, and ended the call.

'Was that Rita?' she asked.

'Nope—my boss. Who sends his best wishes, by the way. Rita sends her love and says on no account are you to even think about coming back to work until the middle of next week. And before you start worrying, she says that if anyone asks, she's going to tell them you're off with a gastric bug.'

'So what now?'

'We've both got a week off.'

'Both?'

'I'm owed some time. My vote is, we get an appointment with a specialist. And then we go away for a few days.'

'Where?'

'Anywhere that doesn't have memories.' His face was grim. 'Right now I don't want to be here—I don't want to walk past the door of the nursery and think of what might have been. So I'm guessing it's worse for you.'

She felt the tears well up again. 'Yes. But going away…isn't that just trying to run from it all?'

'No. It's giving us some space and distance—so when we come back we're feeling stronger and able to deal with the situation. Together,' he emphasised.

'You've taken time off? But you're really busy at work, Alex.'

He shrugged. 'You're more important.' He paused. 'It seems that as of last week, I get private healthcare as part of the package at work, and because you're my wife that includes you. I was thinking, it might be a way for us to get a faster appointment—unless you'd rather talk to your family doctor?'

She thought about it. 'We need answers. The sooner, the better.'

He nodded. 'Then I'll make the call.' He pushed his chair back. 'But I'd be a hell of a lot happier if you were sitting here with me.'

Taking her cue, she sat on his lap. Slid her arms round his neck. Held him close.

Five minutes later, it was all sorted.

'Tomorrow morning. Which in some ways is very, very bad timing. Our appointment's when we should've been somewhere else.' He kissed the end of her nose. 'But in another way, at least we're going to be doing something positive at ten o'clock. Not just sitting here looking at each other, wishing things were different.'

'Thank you, Alex.' She rested her head on his shoulder. 'You're being brilliant about this.'

'I'm feeling pretty helpless, actually,' he admitted. 'Because nothing I do or say is going to change things.'

'You're here,' she said softly. And he'd put her first. Hadn't walked away, as Gary had. 'And that really, really helps.'

'Good.' He kissed her lightly. 'And I'll hold your hand through everything, tomorrow.'

CHAPTER SIXTEEN

THE appointment was a blur. But at least it wasn't at the same hospital they would've been at for the scan, Isobel thought. The doctor asked all kinds of questions about her medical history, took detailed notes and did an internal examination, and all the way through Alex held her hand, letting her know he was there to support her. He was there during the scans— and it took every ounce of strength she had not to bawl her eyes out, wishing they were having the scan they'd been supposed to have—and squeezed her hand comfortingly while phial after phial of blood was taken.

And then all they had to do was wait for the results.

'This is worse than waiting for exam results,' Isobel said when they'd left the hospital.

'Because at least you have an idea how you've done in an exam, and this is out of our control?' Alex asked.

She nodded. 'So I need to go back to work, Alex. I'm going to go crazy if I spend the whole of the next week just waiting with nothing to occupy my mind.'

'I've got a better idea,' Alex said. 'Let's go away for a few days. How do you fancy Florence?'

'What—now?'

'Why not? It's not going to take long to pack. And if we're

wandering round churches and museums and piazzas, we'll be too busy exploring to worry.'

He had a point. 'Thank you.' She paused. 'But, um, it's not going to be like a honeymoon. You heard what the doctor said. No sex for the next month.'

Alex smiled. 'There's more to a marriage than sex. Besides, he didn't actually say "no sex"—just that we shouldn't try for a baby until after your next period. Which, quite apart from the fact we're waiting for your blood test results, is common sense.'

Clearly she still looked worried, because he laced his fingers through hers. 'Relax, Bel. We don't have to have full sex. But we can do an awful lot of other things.' He grinned. 'We can pretend we're teenagers again. Do all the things we maybe should've done twelve years ago.'

'It wouldn't have worked, twelve years ago,' she pointed out.

'You had a world to conquer—and I still had a fair bit of growing up to do. Full of testosterone and not enough finesse.' He stole a kiss. 'I love you, Isobel Richardson. And we don't have to have sex until you're ready. I can be patient.'

She smiled. 'Alex, you've never been patient. You live your life at a hundred miles an hour.'

'For you,' he said, 'I can be patient. Because you're worth it.'

And he proved it. They spent the next week in Florence, wandering round the piazzas, churches and galleries, hand in hand. And on the moments when she went quiet and still inside, thinking of the baby they'd lost and the might-have-beens, he was there to hold her. To whisper that he loved her, and that it was going to work out.

And then it was Friday and they were back for the test results.

Alex paused at the doorway to the hospital. 'Whatever the doctor says to us, remember that I love you and nothing, but *nothing*, is going to change that.' He drew Isobel's hands up to his mouth and kissed the backs of her fingers.

'I love you, too,' Isobel whispered.

The specialist smiled at them when they were ushered in. 'I'm going to need you to have another blood test in about six weeks, Mrs Richardson, before I can give you an absolute diagnosis—but, given what you've told me about your previous miscarriages all being around the ten to twelve week mark and the headaches you had as a teenager, I'm pretty sure that you have antiphospholipid syndrome.'

'What's that?' Isobel asked.

'It's an autoimmune disorder—your immune system is fighting your body and attacking the good tissues, and the antibodies make your blood "sticky" so it clots more than the average person's. It causes miscarriage because clots form in the placenta and the foetus doesn't get enough blood supply.'

'So it *was* my fault.' Isobel swallowed hard.

Alex's hand tightened round hers, telling her silently that she wasn't to blame herself and he still loved her regardless.

'It's not your fault,' the consultant said quietly. 'It's a medical condition. The symptoms are common to a lot of other conditions, so without the antiphospholipid test you wouldn't even know you had it.'

'So what causes it?' Alex asked. 'Is it a virus?'

'We don't know completely,' the specialist said, 'though we do know there's a genetic component. Do you know if anyone else in your family has had recurrent miscarriages, Mrs Richardson?'

'Not for definite,' Isobel said, 'though I'm an only child and, reading between the lines, my parents tried for a very long while before they had me.'

'Then there may be a link there.' He smiled at them both. 'The good news is that it's the most common treatable cause of recurrent miscarriage. As I said, I need you to come back for another test in about six weeks to confirm it, but your other tests are all clear. Your blood pressure's fine and there's no problem with your cervix. So when we've done the second test, if it confirms what I think right now, we'll start treating you and you can go ahead and try for another baby.'

'That's fantastic,' Alex said. 'What's the treatment?'

'One junior aspirin a day.'

Isobel wasn't quite sure she'd heard him right. 'One junior aspirin a day?' she queried.

'That's right. I know it sounds a simple thing, but it works. It'll be enough to thin your blood—and it'll quadruple your chances of having a successful pregnancy.'

'One junior aspirin a day,' she said, just to check.

He nodded. 'And we'll keep a close eye on you through-out the pregnancy. We'll give you more frequent scans so we can keep an eye on the baby, but all the odds are on your side.'

Alex turned to Isobel, his eyes lit with relief. 'Everything's going to be just fine.'

'If the second test confirms it,' she reminded him.

He smiled. 'It will.'

Alex still travelled over the next few weeks, but made a point of not being away for more than one night at a time. And he called her while he was away.

'I miss you,' he said.

'I miss you, too,' she admitted.

'I bought you a present today.'

'Oh?' she enquired, responding to the teasing note in his voice.

'Uh-huh. It's an incredibly sexy nightie.'

She remembered their wedding night. 'It had better not be silk, given what you do to silk things!'

He laughed. 'No, it's the softest, softest jersey. And it'll cling to your curves—have I told you how much I love your curves, Isobel?'

'Indeed, Mr Richardson.'

'Anyway. It's got these little spaghetti straps. And when I get home I'm really looking forward to seeing you try it on.'

'Are you giving me a dirty phone call, Alex?' she teased.

'Might be. What are you wearing?'

She laughed. 'Jeans and a T-shirt. Or is this where I'm meant to do a Marilyn Monroe and say I'm only wearing Chanel No. 5?'

He laughed back. 'That's not the perfume you wear. And I have to say, Mrs Richardson, your perfume is much, much sexier.' He paused. 'If you want to lose the jeans and T-shirt and go to bed while you're talking to me, honey, that's fine by me.'

So he *was* giving her a dirty phone call. 'Where are you, Alex?'

'In my hotel room. With a big empty bed, and I'm missing my wife. Especially as I really, really want to see her in this nightie. Have I told you there's a lot of lace, as well? And the best bit is, because it's jersey, it stretches. I can slide the straps off your shoulders, then push it down, so I can see you and touch you and kiss you and…' He paused teasingly.

She could imagine the scenario and her mouth went dry. 'Oh, yes?'

'Mmm. As I'm miles away, I can't do what I want to do, right now…but I can tell you, Bel.' His voice went husky. 'I can tell you exactly what I'm going to do to you tomorrow night when I come home.'

He did.

In detail.

And by the time he'd finished, she was quivering. 'You'd better deliver on this tomorrow night, Alex,' she warned. 'Because right now I feel as if I'm going to spontaneously combust.'

'Tomorrow night,' he promised, 'we both are.'

The week between her second test and getting the results seemed to stretch for ever. But finally it was confirmed that the problem was antiphospholipid syndrome.

'So tonight we're going to celebrate,' Alex said, holding her close. 'Everything's going to be all right now. You just wait.'

Three weeks later, Isobel called Alex—who was working from home—in her afternoon break. 'Alex, I'm late.'

'OK. Call me when you get to the station and I'll start cooking dinner. Something quick—a stirfry or something.'

'No, not that sort of late. *Late*.'

There was a pause while he digested what she was saying. 'How late?'

'Half a day. But, Alex, I'm regular to the hour.'

'When are you going to be home?' he asked.

'About half past six.'

'Good. And, Bel?'

'Yes?'

'It doesn't matter if it doesn't happen this month. It's still early days and we have plenty of time.'

'Uh-huh.' Though whatever the test said, she knew she was going to be on edge. Horribly disappointed if it was negative, and terrified if it was positive, just in case the specialist was wrong and the aspirin wasn't enough and she'd miscarry again.

When she walked in the door, Alex greeted her with a hug and a warm, sweet kiss. 'OK?' he asked.

'Yes. No.' She bit her lip. 'I've been dying to do a test all day. But I wanted to wait until I was home with you.'

He produced a box. 'Is this one OK?'

She looked at it and smiled. 'Snap.' She produced an identical box from her handbag.

'Great minds think alike,' he quipped. 'Bel—remember what I said. It's early days. If it's negative, that's OK. We just get the fun of trying for another month.'

But she wasn't going to repeat the mistake she'd made in her last marriage. 'I'm not going to make love to you only to make babies,' she said softly. 'It'll be because I love you.'

'Good. I love you, too.' He kissed her lingeringly. 'Now go to the bathroom. I've been clock-watching all afternoon and I can't wait another minute.'

'What was that line you fed me about being a patient man?' she teased.

But she returned two minutes later. 'One line. So we know the test is working.'

Together, they watched the second window. And as the second blue line appeared, Isobel buried her face in Alex's chest and bawled her eyes out.

'It's going to be OK this time,' he said softly, stroking her hair.

'I'm not crying because I'm upset. I'm crying because I'm relieved. Because I'm happy.' But she kept her arms wrapped very tightly round him. 'Alex. I don't want to tell anyone yet.'

'Of course not.'

'Not until twelve weeks.'

He nuzzled her cheek. 'I know you're scared, but it's different this time. We know what the problem was and you're doing everything you should be,' he reassured her. 'But we'll get you an appointment tomorrow and we're going to keep an eye on you. And I promise you, I'm not going to work away from home for the next few months.'

'Alex, that's not fair. You have a job to do.'

'I'm not taking any risks,' he said softly. 'I promised you that you'd come first. And you do.' He held her close. 'And this time everything's going to be fine.'

EPILOGUE

Nine months later

ALEX and Isobel sat on the edge of the bed, watching their daughter sleeping in the Moses basket next to their bed. Her first night home. Their first night in the Bloomsbury flat as a family.

'She's so perfect,' Isobel said. 'I can still hardly believe she's ours.'

'Thea. Gift of God,' he translated softly. 'Dad's still campaigning for us to call her Thomasina, you know. And your dad's desperately trying to find a feminine version of Stuart. And Saskia's put in her bid for the middle name as well as begging to be godmother.'

Isobel laughed. 'Thea isn't being named after anyone. She's just herself.'

'Though she's as beautiful as her mother.' Alex, with one arm firmly round his wife's shoulders, reached out to stroke his daughter's cheek with the tip of his finger. 'My two beautiful girls. Life doesn't get any better than this, Bel.' He rested his head against Isobel's.

'I never knew I could be this happy,' she said softly. 'But with you, I have the whole world. A job I love, the baby I've wanted for so long…and, most of all, you. I love you, Alex.'

'I love you, too,' he said softly. *'Semper.'*

Demure but defiant...
Can three international playboys
tame their disobedient brides?

Lynne Graham

presents

Virgin BRIDES ♥ Arrogant HUSBANDS

Proud, masculine and passionate, these men are used
to having it all. In stories filled with drama, desire
and secrets of the past, find out how these arrogant
husbands capture their hearts.

THE GREEK TYCOON'S DISOBEDIENT BRIDE

Available December 2008, Book #2779

THE RUTHLESS MAGNATE'S VIRGIN MISTRESS

Available January 2009, Book #2787

THE SPANISH BILLIONAIRE'S PREGNANT WIFE

Available February 2009, Book #2795

www.eHarlequin.com

HP12787

EXTRA

HIRED: FOR THE BOSS'S PLEASURE

She's gone from personal assistant
to mistress—but now he's demanding
she become the boss's bride!

Read all our fabulous stories this month:

MISTRESS: HIRED FOR THE BILLIONAIRE'S PLEASURE
by INDIA GREY

THE BILLIONAIRE BOSS'S INNOCENT BRIDE
by LINDSAY ARMSTRONG

HER RUTHLESS ITALIAN BOSS
by CHRISTINA HOLLIS

MEDITERRANEAN BOSS, CONVENIENT MISTRESS
by KATHRYN ROSS

www.eHarlequin.com

HPE0209

*Life is a game of power and pleasure.
And these men play to win!*

Let Harlequin Presents® take you on a jet-set journey
to meet eight male wonders of the world. From rich
tycoons to royal playboys— they're red-hot and ruthless!

International Billionaires coming in 2009

THE PRINCE'S WAITRESS WIFE
by *Sarah Morgan*, February

AT THE ARGENTINEAN BILLIONAIRE'S BIDDING
by *India Grey*, March

THE FRENCH TYCOON'S PREGNANT MISTRESS
by *Abby Green*, April

THE RUTHLESS BILLIONAIRE'S VIRGIN
by *Susan Stephens*, May

THE ITALIAN COUNT'S DEFIANT BRIDE
by *Catherine George*, June

THE SHEIKH'S LOVE-CHILD
by *Kate Hewitt*, July

BLACKMAILED INTO THE GREEK TYCOON'S BED
by *Carol Marinelli*, August

THE VIRGIN SECRETARY'S IMPOSSIBLE BOSS
by *Carol Mortimer*, September

8 volumes in all to collect!

www.eHarlequin.com

HP12798

REQUEST YOUR
FREE BOOKS!

2 FREE NOVELS
PLUS 2
FREE GIFTS!

YES! Please send me 2 FREE Harlequin Presents® novels and my 2 FREE gifts (gifts are worth about $10). After receiving them, if I don't wish to receive any more books, I can return the shipping statement marked "cancel". If I don't cancel, I will receive 6 brand-new novels every month and be billed just $4.05 per book in the U.S. or $4.74 per book in Canada, plus 25¢ shipping and handling per book and applicable taxes, if any*. That's a savings of close to 15% off the cover price! I understand that accepting the 2 free books and gifts places me under no obligation to buy anything. I can always return a shipment and cancel at any time. Even if I never buy another book, the two free books and gifts are mine to keep forever.   106 HDN ERRW 306 HDN ERRL

Name _____ (PLEASE PRINT) _____

Address _____ Apt. # _____

City _____ State/Prov. _____ Zip/Postal Code _____

Signature (if under 18, a parent or guardian must sign)

Mail to the **Harlequin Reader Service:**
IN U.S.A.: P.O. Box 1867, Buffalo, NY 14240-1867
IN CANADA: P.O. Box 609, Fort Erie, Ontario L2A 5X3

Not valid to current subscribers of Harlequin Presents books.

Want to try two free books from another line?
Call 1-800-873-8635 or visit www.morefreebooks.com.

* Terms and prices subject to change without notice. N.Y. residents add applicable sales tax. Canadian residents will be charged applicable provincial taxes and GST. Offer not valid in Quebec. This offer is limited to one order per household. All orders subject to approval. Credit or debit balances in a customer's account(s) may be offset by any other outstanding balance owed by or to the customer. Please allow 4 to 6 weeks for delivery. Offer available while quantities last.

Your Privacy: Harlequin Books is committed to protecting your privacy. Our Privacy Policy is available online at www.eHarlequin.com or upon request from the Reader Service. From time to time we make our lists of customers available to reputable third parties who may have a product or service of interest to you. If you would prefer we not share your name and address, please check here. ☐

HP08R

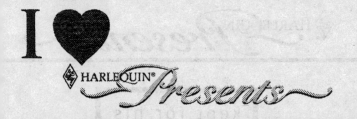

I ♥ HARLEQUIN Presents

BROUGHT TO YOU BY FANS OF
HARLEQUIN PRESENTS.

We are its editors and authors
and biggest fans—and we'd
love to hear from YOU!

Subscribe today to our online blog at
www.iheartpresents.com

kept for his *Pleasure*

She's his mistress on demand!

Wherever seduction takes place, these fabulously
wealthy, charismatic, sexy men know how to
keep a woman coming back for more!

She's his mistress on demand—but when he
wants her body *and soul* he will be demanding
a whole lot more! Dare we say it…even marriage!

CONFESSIONS OF A
MILLIONAIRE'S MISTRESS
by **Robyn Grady**

**Don't miss any books in
this exciting new miniseries
from Harlequin Presents!**

www.eHarlequin.com

HP12801